DEADBEAT

Published by:
Hollygrove Publishing, Inc.
4100 West Eldorado Parkway
Suite 100-182
McKinney, Texas 75070
(972) 837-6191
http://www.hollygrovepublishing.com
http://www.facebook.com/HollygrovePublishing

10 - Digit ISBN: 0-9840904-4-4
13 – Digit ISBN: 978-0-9840904-4-0

Printed in the United States of America

Publisher's Note
This is a work of fiction. All events in this story are solely the product of the Author's imagination. Any similarities between any characters and situations in this book to any individuals, living or dead, or actual places and situations are purely coincidental.

DEADBEAT

BY

Brian W. Smith

TAKING READING TO ANOTHER LEVEL!

"Everyone has a story… even homeless people."

Brian W. Smith

Chapter 1

The left front wheel on the rickety shopping cart being pushed by the homeless man was damaged so badly it looked as if it would fall off at any moment. Pebbles were disintegrated as the dragging wheel slid across the concrete, while the other three bore the brunt of the weight from the contents of the cart.

The man pushing the cart ignored the faulty wheel the same way he ignored the flies hovering around his head and the despair surrounding him; men arguing over whose turn it was to take a sip from the whiskey bottle; an unkempt woman sitting on an old crate talking to herself; the stench of urine lingering in the air creating a smell that was tolerable, but definitely unfavorable.

With laser like focus he kept pushing his cart down the dusty path that parted the homeless community like a long suburban street. He masterfully kept one eye on the contents of his mobile home while his other eye surveyed his surroundings watching out for thieves looking to steal some of his valuables.

The temperature was inching towards ninety degrees on this humid day in New Orleans, but that didn't seem to faze the determined cart pusher. He wore a soiled black knitted cap to cover his nappy hair. With his beard matted on his cheeks and chin, he resembled Marvin Gaye during his *Let's Get It On* days in the 70's.

His overcoat was tattered and missing several buttons. It was dark brown and stained so badly that black blotches on the lapel and sleeves could be seen from ten feet away.

Once a vacant space was identified, he stopped his journey and looked around to see if anyone was rushing over to lay claim to the spot.

"Hey, my man," said his homeless neighbor. The plump white man, with a beard that reached down to the center of his chest, was obviously a regular who knew the do's and don'ts of that area.

"Hey... is this spot taken?"

"Nope," replied the Santa Claus look alike. "It's yours if you want it. Watch your stuff, these little wild ass kids are all over the place today."

The city's less fortunate could be seen for nearly two blocks in the area commonly referred to as Tent City. Located on Claiborne Avenue, city officials turned a blind eye to the indigent sub-culture that had sprung up just a little more than a mile from the touristy Bourbon Street area. Homeless people spent the bulk of their days within this four block stretch nesting in flimsy tents or card board boxes manipulated to provide shelter.

A few feet away, a slim girl wearing jeans that were so tight she'd need to use a tub of grease to slide out of them, walked past. She was being hounded by an overbearing teenage boy.

"Come here, girl! You need to stop playin' and give a nigga your phone number," said Bookie, the teenage boy who was unsuccessfully pursuing the girl.

Dexter "Bookie" Howard was a short thin framed, hot tempered 15 year old. He was one of those kids that stayed in so much trouble even the most patient adults would lose their cool after more than thirty minutes in his presence. This kid couldn't spell tact, let alone display it. He had an attitude that was destined to lead him down the path of incarceration or an early death.

Sigmund Freud theorized that, *The ego expels whatever within itself that becomes a source of displeasure.* Bookie's constant rejection made him feel smaller than his physical stature displayed. Picking fights was his way of lashing out at the world. His photo should have been listed in the dictionary next to the phrase, *Napoleon Complex.*

"What y'all lookin' at?" Bookie shouted, after he realized that his failed attempt at courting the young girl had been witnessed by many of the itinerant citizens who called Tent City their home.

"What you lookin' at old man?" Bookie asked, singling out the long bearded homeless man.

The man wisely didn't reply. He simply turned, looked down at the ground, and staggered away. As with most impoverished areas in major cities, the rules of survival are simple: mind your own business; don't start a fight you can't finish; mind your own business; and most importantly, mind your own business.

Experience had taught the homeless onlookers that pretending to ignore the juvenile delinquency swirling around them was a sure way to extend their life expectancy.

While Bookie looked around for some other indigent person to pick on, his partners in crime, Tweety and QJ, were a block away talking and eating their evening meals.

Interstate 10, the major thoroughfare that residents of the city used to travel from the eastern part of the city to the western suburbs, is propped in the air by massive concrete columns that look like they were plucked from a Roman coliseum. They stretched for miles.

Keeping an interstate from tumbling was the most obvious use of these concrete behemoths, but they were used for other creative purposes. Inebriated party goers used the columns as something to lean against during Mardi Gras. People with a proclivity for urinating in the streets used them to hide behind while they took a quick bathroom break. The columns were even put to good use by vandals and graffiti artist looking for a smooth surface to express themselves.

On this particular day, Tweety and QJ were posted up against one of the columns devouring foot long po'boy sandwiches and discussing the events of the day.

The intersection of Claiborne Avenue and Canal Street may have seemed like an odd place to eat a meal, but it was the normal chow down spot for these rowdy teens. It was their gathering spot after school. The place where they laughed, lied, and flirted with the girls who lived in the Iberville projects as they passed.

The honking horns and police sirens that seem to blare incessantly, served as the soundtrack to their lives. The troubled teenage boys were oblivious to the poverty and despair surrounding them as they basked in their youth.

Suddenly, their meals and tête-à-tête were interrupted by a familiar sound – Bookie engaged in a scuffle.

"Get off me!" Bookie shouted in a tone that sounded more like a high pitch squeal. The fear in his voice could be heard over the evening traffic. "Y'all, come help me! This fool is tryin' to kill me!"

"C'mon, Bookie's in trouble," Tweety bellowed as he tossed his sandwich to the side, and started pouring the remainder of his coke out on the ground. He ran to Bookie's rescue like an Olympic sprinter with the finish line in sight.

QJ on the other hand, didn't seem to be as eager to throw away his food. He'd been craving a hot sausage po'boy on French bread all day. He was about 2/3 of the way into it when Bookie started screaming like a little sissy.

"C'mon, QJ!" Tweety shouted as he got closer to Bookie.

"I'm comin'... damn!" QJ replied as he stuffed a chunk of the sandwich into his mouth. "This is the best part. I'll be damned if I'm going to throw my food away!"

He took one last swig of his pineapple-flavored soda, and then jogged towards the mêlée. It wasn't that he was scared to scrap, but he knew his friends better than anyone. QJ had no idea why Bookie was getting his butt whipped, but he knew Bookie probably started the fight.

Bookie was the smallest one in their clique, but he had the biggest mouth. It seemed like every week Tweety and QJ were coming to his rescue, and QJ was getting tired of it. Tweety on the other hand, got a kick out of it.

QJ's jog turned into an all out sprint once he saw what appeared to be a grown man slam Bookie's little 5'6" frame up against one of those columns. Bookie's jaws shimmied and his teeth rattled as his under-developed body smashed against the immoveable object.

The man followed his WWF-style body slam with a right hook that hit Bookie flush in the eye. It all looked like the scene from the movie *Cooley High* when Cochise was getting beat up under the bridge.

"Get the fuck off him!" Tweety shouted, and then smashed the coke bottle against the side of the man's head.

Bookie's attacker was the homeless man with the defective shopping cart. The man released his grip of Bookie and slumped to the ground, his hands clasping the right side of his head and ear.

Dazed from the beating he'd taken, Bookie slid down the column and landed on the seat of his pants. Blood spewed from a fresh wound above his left eyebrow like water flowing from a faucet.

Tweety was too busy unleashing a barrage of blows to the head and rib cage of the grungy-looking man to notice Bookie was in need of serious medical attention.

"He tried to take my cart!" the man shouted as he lay curled up in a fetal position struggling to protect himself from Tweety's attack. "I didn't want to hit him. He tried to take my stuff!"

The man's pleas for mercy were futile. He was about to get the type of ass-whooping reserved for child molesters.

QJ helped Bookie stand up. The sleeve of his shirt was now covered in Bookie's blood. Once it was clear to him that his injured friend could stand on his own, the two of them commenced to helping Tweety with the beat down.

Bookie grabbed a piece of concrete that appeared to have broken off from the base of the column. The chunk of concrete was smooth on top, but had jagged edges. It was so large Bookie had to use two hands to pick it up.

"Leave him alone!" shouted a wrinkled rundown looking homeless woman as she peeped out of her cardboard house. "Y'all leave him alone!"

"Fuck you!" shouted Bookie.

It would take more than a feeble request from a homeless woman to douse this rage. Bookie's attention quickly shifted from that woman to the man who'd just split his eyebrow open.

QJ looked around and spotted a lead pipe a few feet away from the homeless woman's quarters.

"Move Tweety!" barked Bookie. "Let me at this fool!"

Tweety was so engaged in beating the man that he was pissed at Bookie for wanting to get some of the action. Bookie lifted the huge piece of concrete above his head, and then smashed it down on the man's side.

The helpless man let out a wail that was so gut wrenching even QJ cringed. From where QJ stood, the homeless man looked like a pile of blood-stained, dirty clothes.

"Nigga, come get some!" Tweety shouted, as he looked in QJ's direction.

QJ was usually the ring leader in their throw downs with rival fake thugs, but something about this was wrong—real wrong.

"Come get some, QJ!" shouted Tweety again, as he and Bookie kicked the man in any part of his body that was exposed.

"Don't do it, baby," the homeless woman pleaded as she looked at QJ.

Her appearance didn't command respect, but her tone did. It was the tone God reserved for grandmothers. The type of tone that would cause even the most hardened thug to pause, and at least reconsider his actions.

Unfortunately, at the age of fifteen, QJ didn't have the maturity needed to identify when one of God's angels was speaking to him. He looked at the woman, and then tightened his grip on the pipe in his hand.

Just as his better judgment was about to kick in, QJ heard Bookie utter the one phrase that has prompted level-headed teenage boys across this country to make stupid decisions.

"Tweety, that nigga QJ scared!"

Whatever common sense QJ possessed left him the moment he heard Bookie attack his manhood.

"Scared?" QJ replied. "Nigga, move out of the way!"

QJ could barely see the man's face. The entire right side of the victim's head was drenched in blood. When Bookie and Tweety backed away, the man struggled to his feet.

"Knock his ass out!" shouted Tweety.

QJ gripped the pipe in his right hand and cocked back. He was so nervous his palms became sweaty, causing him to nearly drop the pipe.

In an attempt to make the boys stop their attack, onlookers honked their car horns and shouted, "Leave him alone!" They may have been outraged at the scene, but that was the extent of their intervention. The fear of becoming a victim too was enough to deter any physical intercession.

Tweety and Bookie were defiant throughout. They flipped the bird and mockingly grabbed their crotches to show their lack of concern at anyone who dared to get involved.

"Hurry up!" shouted Bookie. "I can hear the police coming."

Bookie was right. Police sirens were getting closer. Traffic on Claiborne Avenue had come to a halt. In between the concrete columns that kept the interstate from crumbling and the cars that aligned the street, QJ could see the blue lights from the police car heading their way.

"C'mon QJ, bust his ass so we can go!" Tweety commanded, as he and Bookie started to back pedal. When QJ turned and looked back at them they were nearly jogging in the other direction.

"Don't do it son," said the homeless man.

"Shut yo ass up!" QJ retorted. "You split my boy's eye. I'm about to split yo head!"

"I only hit him because he tried to steal my stuff," the man said. "The stuff in that cart is all I got... since I lost you, QJ."

Time seemed to stand still as QJ stood there with a perplexed look on his face. He thought he heard the man say, "since I lost you, QJ."

Apparently QJ's facial expression reflected his bewilderment. He could feel his anger grow as he looked into the begging eyes of the bleeding homeless man.

"What did you just say?"

"You heard me, son. It's me – your daddy."

"What?" QJ shouted. "Ma'fucka, my daddy's dead!"

"I'm not dead, QJ," the man replied, as he tried to speak while spitting out the blood that had gathered in his mouth along with a tooth that had been jarred loose by one of the blows he'd received.

"Man, I'm gonna split yo head!"

The man continued to plead for his life. "I'm Quincy – your daddy. Your mama's name is Carmen. They call her Cookie. I'm the one who gave her that nickname when she was pregnant with you. All she ate during her pregnancy were cookies. That's when I started callin' her Cookie."

At that moment, QJ's facial expression looked as if he was the one who'd been getting his ass beaten. Suddenly his knees became weak. His heart started to pound so hard he thought it was going to burst through his shirt.

The more he stared at the homeless man, the more he realized that he and the victim standing before him shared the same facial features. Their skin complexion was identical. They had the same thick eyebrows. They both had noses that were so wide they seemed to span the width of their faces. Only a DNA connection could explain the similarity in their thick, often-chapped lips. QJ thought he was seeing a ghost.

"Daddy—is that you?"

"Yes, son. It's me. Please don't do this."

"Run, QJ!" shouted Tweety, as he and Bookie turned and dashed up the street.

QJ looked over the shoulder of this man claiming to be his father. The police officers had exited their vehicle, and were running towards them. Suddenly, the man who stood before QJ transformed from his potential victim into his protector.

"Run, son," he said.

The boy could feel a lump develop in his throat. His abdominal muscles tightened. Sweat beads begin to form on his forehead. A battle was taking place inside of him. It was a battle between his ego and his common sense.

"Go that way," Quincy said, and pointed across the street. "Run down that alley over there. It will lead you into the projects. Once you get in the projects they won't be able to find you."

There was a unique tone in Quincy's voice; the tone that God reserves for caring fathers. The anger that had a strangle hold on QJ's emotions just a few seconds earlier dissipated. He felt tamed—like a child who'd just received guidance from his father.

"Hey you!" shouted the cop.

"Run, son. Run, QJ."

QJ's fifteen year old legs felt like they were mired in concrete. Eventually he found the strength to run. He dropped the pipe, and started his escape. He ran with the fervor of a runaway slave.

QJ followed his father's instructions. He darted across the street, dodging cars like a running back trying to make his way through the toughest defense. The boy didn't stop running until he was two courtyards deep into the projects.

When he was almost certain he was no longer being followed he stopped to catch his breath. While he surveyed his surroundings, the scared child sat on the steps of an abandoned project building and tried to regain his composure.

I can't believe that's my daddy. Mama told me he was dead.

QJ's perspiration-soaked shirt was clinging to his chest. He could feel a bead of sweat as it trickled down the center of his forehead, and made its way along the bridge of his nose. Eventually, that sweat bead got tired of dangling from his nose and finally rested on the whiskers covering his top lip.

My dad is a homeless man. Why did she lie? I almost killed him.

He looked up and saw a few ladies perched in their second floor windows looking down at him. Their presence didn't bother QJ. He understood life in the environment he was being raised in. The practice of peeking out the window to investigate the sound of fleeing men was commonplace for women eager to see if one of their relatives was running from the long arm of the law.

Although QJ was concerned about the police and their chase, a weird feeling came over the undisciplined child. For the first time in his life he felt safe; thanks to the quick thinking of his father—Quincy.

Chapter 2

"Someone from the school called today," said Terry in an agitated tone. "It appears your precious son ditched school again. That's the third time this month."

The hair on the back of Carmen's neck stood up whenever she had to listen to Terry make a sarcastic remark about QJ. Her efforts to get the two of them to bond were a total waste of time. QJ and Terry seemed disinterested in removing the tension that stood between them.

The tension was usually fueled by some type of disciplinary related issue. Terry was raised in a strict military household where discipline and superior work ethic were preached excessively. Corporal Punishment was the only method of discipline used. Any form of disrespect was dealt with severely.

Carmen on the other hand, was raised in the foster care system. She learned how to survive, but since she was never an unruly child, she was somewhat unfamiliar with various disciplinary tactics.

Carmen married QJ's father, Quincy, when she was twenty years old. One year later, they were the proud parents of a bouncing baby boy whom they affectionately called QJ, short for Quincy Nathaniel Washington Jr.

Initially, Quincy embraced fatherhood with a zeal that was matched by few. During the days following QJ's birth, Quincy would nearly knock Carmen down as he leaped out of bed in the wee hours of the morning to see why QJ was crying. Watching Quincy operate in the kitchen during bottle preparation was like watching a mad scientist in his lab.

He took warming bottles as seriously as a chemist experimenting with a new concoction. Analyzing the bottle through the microwave window as it turned round and round. Demanding silence as he allowed droplets of warmed milk to splash on his wrist so he could test the temperature. Watching him take a quick sip from the nipple to make sure the milk was *QJ worthy* was a thing of beauty. The way he swished the milk around his mouth and looked up at the ceiling while he concentrated would have made the most ardent wine connoisseur feel like a novice.

   Quincy's enthusiasm for fatherhood became less apparent by QJ's third birthday. Marital problems and an escalating alcohol and drug dependency seemed to be at the root of Quincy's disinterest. The more his distrust in Carmen grew, the more he stayed away from home. The longer he stayed away from home, the greater his proclivity to drink liquor and try harsher drugs. His graduation from weed to crack cocaine seemed to happen overnight.

   As much as she disliked what Quincy had become, Carmen desperately wanted Quincy to maintain an active role in their son's life. Growing up in the foster care system, witnessing kids starving for hands on guidance and attention, enabled Carmen to see the psychological damage done to little black boys forced to grow up without a strong male role model. She was determined to make her child's youth less traumatic—even if it meant staying with a man she no longer respected, desired, or loved.

   QJ's fifth birthday was the day before his first day of elementary school. Carmen and Quincy thought it would be a good idea to celebrate the occasion with a party for QJ. Carmen gave Quincy forty dollars and sent him to the store to pick up the cake she'd ordered and some last minute items for the party. Quincy didn't return for three days.

   When he finally walked back through the front door, it was clear that he was aware of the trauma he'd caused. It was also clear to Carmen that he didn't care. The two of them managed to co-exist for a few more months before another incident occurred; an incident that would bring an abrupt end to their marriage.

Without any forewarning, Quincy packed a bag full of clothes, a large bottle of Hennessey he had in the cabinet, tip-toed into QJ's bedroom and kissed the child on his forehead, and then left the house. A decade would pass before he would come face-to-face with his son again.

During Quincy's ten year absence, Carmen was saddled with the unenviable task of trying to raise a boy on her own in a city that consistently ranked amongst the most crime riddled cities in the United States.

Ironically, Carmen and Terry first met as a result of Quincy. Prior to the birthday party fiasco, she started sensing that Quincy's lifestyle would lead to destruction. Carmen decided to take out a life insurance policy on Quincy. When she walked through the doors of the insurance company, the first agent to greet her was Terry.

Initially, she and Terry's conversations were solely about life insurance and financial planning. However, it wasn't long before they were meeting up for lunch dates. Insurance discussions eventually gave way to more intimate conversations about life and relationships. As one might expect, those awkward silent moments that pop up during conversations became the feeding ground for long flirtatious gazes.

Once it became clear to her that Quincy wasn't coming back, Carmen took the lock off of her emotions and allowed Terry into her life. Like any good sales rep, Terry seized the opportunity to infiltrate the mind and body of the vulnerable single mother. As the years passed, Carmen started to value Terry's opinion on various topics — including the proper way to raise young QJ.

"Baby, I will deal with QJ when he comes home," Carmen replied, refusing to take her eyes off of the mashed potatoes on her plate.

"That's what you said last week," said Terry, in a tone that dripped with cynicism.

"Terry, please pull up!" Carmen replied, and then dropped her fork onto her plate. "I said I will deal with QJ when he comes home."

Terry was good at a lot of things, but pulling up wasn't one.

"Speaking of coming home, didn't you tell him last week he needed to be in this house no later than 7:00 P.M. on a school night?"

"Yes, baby—I did. I will punish QJ when he comes in. Now, can we just eat dinner without arguing?"

"Yeah, we can eat without arguing, but you'd better deal with that boy before I do."

Ten minutes later, and thirty minutes after his curfew, QJ came strolling through the door.

"You're late... again," said Terry.

QJ walked past the kitchen and acted like he didn't hear Terry. He didn't pause until Carmen called him.

"QJ, come here!"

The boy stopped at the foot of the staircase, let out the most disrespectful sigh he could conjure up, rolled his eyes, and then turned around and went into the kitchen.

"What did I do wrong, now?" he asked rudely.

"You broke your curfew again!" shouted Terry. "Plus, somebody from the school called, again!"

"I wasn't talkin' to you! I was talkin' to my mama!"

"Well, I'm talkin' to you!" Terry barked back.

QJ stood there staring at Terry. If looks could kill, Terry would have been toe-tagged and bagged.

"Boy, you'd better stay in your place," Terry insisted. "If you were my son, I would..."

"That's just it; I'm not your son!" QJ yelled.

"Terry, please!" Carmen shouted. "I told you I would handle this."

DEADBEAT — Brian W. Smith

Carmen stood and grabbed QJ's elbow with the same type of grip the young boy had while holding that pipe earlier. She led her rebellious teen up the stairs and into his bedroom. Once the door slammed behind them she commenced to letting QJ have it.

"Boy, what has gotten into you? You never used to be this bad-mannered. Now you're ditching school. You walk around here with your pants sagging off your ass. And I know you're still hanging out with those little criminals— Bookie and Tweety. You're even disrespecting me and Terry. You act like..."

"Fuck Terry!" QJ blurted out.

The words echoed throughout the tiny bedroom, reverberating off the walls until they eventually smacked Carmen upside the head.

Before QJ could get another word out, Carmen had cocked back her arm and slapped the boy so hard across his face that she broke a finger nail.

QJ staggered backwards and grabbed his face. He sat on his bed for a moment and then leaned backwards and buried his head in the pillow. Carmen was furious.

"Boy, as long as you live in my house, you will respect me and my rules. Do you understand me?"

QJ didn't answer.

"Quincy Washington Jr.!" she shouted. "Do you hear me?" QJ still didn't answer. His failure to respond caused his mother's anger to grow. She looked around the room and spotted a belt on a nearby chair. Carmen grabbed the belt and headed towards QJ. He was going to acknowledge her even if she had to beat it out of him. Fortunately for him, he responded just as she was about to start wailing on him.

"Why did you lie?"

Carmen paused long enough to reply, "What?"

QJ removed his head from his pillow and asked, "Why did you lie to me about my daddy?"

Carmen instantly knew where her son's line of questioning was heading. She immediately decided to pretend she didn't know what QJ was talking about. But her facial expression told it all.

"You told me my daddy was dead," the angry boy continued.

"He is dead," Carmen replied hesitantly.

"Stop lying to me!" QJ shouted. "I know you're lying. I met him today. Why did you lie to me all these years?"

Carmen and QJ's conversation was muffled since the bedroom door was closed, but the silence was driving Terry crazy.

"Baby, are you okay in there?" Terry asked from the other side of the door.

Carmen plopped down on her son's bed— flabbergasted. Her eyes immediately filled with water. A lump developed in her throat. She dropped the belt on the floor, and then looked at the bedroom door.

"Umm, we're fine baby. Why don't you go ahead and leave. QJ and I are just talking."

"Yeah, leave!" QJ shouted.

Terry punched the door, and walked away. When they heard the front door slam shut, they finished their discussion. By this time, tears were streaming down QJ's cheeks.

Carmen glanced at her son and then looked down at the floor searching for a response to her son's simple, yet extremely complicated question.

"Where did you see your father?"

"I saw him living down in Tent City on Claiborne Avenue. You told me he was dead."

"Are you sure it was him?"

"Yeah, I'm sure!" QJ shouted. "He knew you. He even knew your nickname. He told me he's the one who gave it to you."

QJ's words seem to cut through Carmen's heart like a hot knife cuts through a stick of butter. Tears were now streaming down her cheeks as she struggled to find the right words to say.

"Why did you lie to me all these years? You told me he got killed in a car wreck while out of town on business. You told me I could never visit his gravesite because the cemetery he was buried at was flooded. You had me believing my daddy was dead, and he lives right here in the same damn city."

Carmen could feel herself start to hyperventilate. She placed her hand over her chest and started taking long, deep breaths. Once she regained her composure she answered her son.

"Baby, I told you your father died because it was easier than telling you the truth."

"What truth?"

"It's complicated."

"Complicated? So complicated that it's easier to say he was dead?"

"QJ, your father left us when you were five years old. He had a real bad drug habit and was out of control. One day he just left and never returned. He left me with the responsibility of taking care of you alone."

"Are you tryin' to say my daddy is a deadbeat?"

Carmen didn't reply. She just reached over and rubbed her son's leg. QJ leaned backwards and stared up at the ceiling.

"So, that punk just walked away and left us hangin'? I'll be damned, all these years I've been thinkin' about that fool, and he ain't nothin' but a bum."

"Baby, your daddy couldn't shake his demons. I know he loved you, but..."

"Man, I don't wanna hear that. I should have split his head open when I had the chance."

"What are you talking about?"

QJ stood and opened his door. Before Carmen could call his name, he was already down the stairs and walking out the front door.

"QJ!" she shouted out. "Where are you going?"

The only reply she got was the sound of the front door slamming. Suddenly, Carmen felt like vomiting, and she did—all over the floor.

It was nearly ten o'clock that night when QJ returned home. He rolled his eyes at the sight of Terry's SUV parked in the driveway.

Man, this ma'fucka is always over here; sucking up our air and in my mama's face.

The creaking sound the front door made when being opened eliminated any possibility of QJ sneaking in the house undetected. His best hope was that his mother and Terry were in the bedroom sleeping. His hopes were dashed when he reached the top of the staircase and saw Terry standing there waiting.

"Where have you been?"

"None of your damn business," QJ replied tersely.

"It became my business when I had to come over here and calm your mama down when she couldn't stop crying because your out of control ass left without telling her where you were going."

Terry grabbed QJ's collar and shoved him up against the wall. Although QJ wasn't a small kid, the nearly one hundred pound weight difference all but ensured the child wasn't going to be able to break away and run.

"You think you're a thug? If I didn't think your mama would hear I'd kick your little ass right now," Terry whispered.

QJ's slender frame was pressed against his bedroom door. He may have been temporarily immobilized, but the look in his eyes was a clear indication he wasn't scared.

"Boy, you'd better get your act together. Your mama and I are gonna be together whether you like it or not, so you may as well get used to it. I'm gonna be moving in here soon, and when I do, some things are gonna change around here."

Terry reached and turned the door knob on QJ's bedroom door. When the door swung open, QJ fell backwards into the room and landed on his butt. Terry stared for a moment, smirked, and then walked down the stairs. The front door slammed a few seconds later—Terry was gone.

QJ was left sitting on the floor in shock. He even paused long enough to get a whiff of the undeniable aroma of vomit that permeated his room. Once he refocused, his fiery temper kicked in. He grabbed a baseball bat that was propped up in the corner of his bedroom. His intent was to inflict pain on Terry, but his momentum was stopped—by his mom.

"Where are you going with that bat?"

"Mama, move."

"I'm not budging. Where are you going with that bat?"

"Mama, I'm tellin' you, you need to move or…"

"Or what? Are you gonna hit me with that bat?"

QJ stood there huffing and puffing like a boxer in between rounds. Before he could reply, Carmen snatched the bat out of his hand.

"You ain't going nowhere. Sit down!"

QJ reluctantly complied. He sat on the edge of his bed, and stared at the adjacent bedroom wall. Carmen placed the bat on the bed, and sat next to her son.

"QJ, I was worried sick. Where did you go?"

"I went for a walk."

"You weren't walking for three hours. Where'd you go?"

QJ didn't answer. He avoided all eye contact with his mother. Carmen's motherly instincts made her question somewhat rhetorical, she knew her son well enough to know exactly where he'd gone.

"QJ, did you go looking for him?"

Her question was initially met with silence. Just as she was about to ask again QJ replied, "Yeah, I went looking for his sorry ass. He's lucky I didn't find him."

Carmen grabbed her son's clinched fist. The two of them sat on the bed for nearly five minutes with her slender fingers engulfing his knuckles. The boy didn't need a lecture, he needed a hug. But, she knew he was still angry at her for lying to him all those years. Rather than drag this emotionally charged scene out any longer, Carmen tried to sooth the savage beast lurking inside of her child by gently rubbing his forehead.

"Baby I know you're angry. I know you have a lot of unanswered questions. I know I owe you a more detailed explanation. I'm gonna give you what you need, but not tonight. It's late and we both need to rest. We can talk about this tomorrow."

Carmen kissed QJ on the forehead and stood up. "Please try to get some rest, and promise me you won't leave again tonight."

QJ didn't answer verbally, but nodded his head. He stretched out on his bed and turned his back to his mom so she couldn't see the tears forming in his eyes.

Carmen fought to hold back her own tears. She turned off the bedroom light and closed the door. The walk back to her room, located two doors down the hall, was a long one. She was exhausted. She was nervous. She was scared. The evening had been a long one, but at least the savage beast within QJ had been tamed—for the time being.

Chapter 3

Carmen blew gently into a cup of hot coffee trying to cool it down. She'd learned her lesson a week earlier when she'd ignored the steam coming from the cup and sipped without blowing. The tip of her tongue was burned so bad she spent the next three days flinching every time she tried to taste anything.

The caramel complexioned, hazel eyed beauty's bout with a cup of decaf took place in Tiny's Diner. Carmen was a regular at the establishment. She'd practically grown up on the steak and eggs breakfast. Because of its proximity to the Central Business District, the hole in the wall diner was a favorite nesting spot for New Orleans police officers, firefighters, and politicians.

Carmen waited patiently for Lawana to appear. While she waited and mulled over the topics she wanted to discuss, Carmen struggled to focus. The clinking of plates, searing of the open grill, and the buzz of multiple patron conversations created a cacophony of sounds that were too distracting to ignore.

Lawana and Carmen met in high school and had been inseparable. She was with Carmen the day she met Quincy. She was the person who drove Carmen to the hospital when she went into labor. She was the person who helped Carmen pay her household bills after Quincy left.

Lawana was sassy, educated, attractive, and free spirited. Sometimes Carmen even wished she was Lawana—often living vicariously through her sprightly friend.

Along with being the safe-guarder of Carmen's deepest secrets, Lawana held two other important titles: 1. QJ's Godmother. 2. the most opinionated woman Carmen knew.

Lawana was that one friend every woman had—she had no kids, but spoke like she knew everything about rearing them. The thing that secretly drove Carmen crazy was that most of the unsolicited advice Lawana offered regarding raising QJ was usually one hundred percent correct.

"Girl, sorry I'm late," said Lawana as she plopped down in the booth. She smelled like DKNY perfume, wore a white silk blouse, skin tight jeans, and was carrying one of her many Gucci handbags.

"What's up, movie star?" asked Carmen sarcastically.

"Movie star? Child please…" Lawana replied.

"You're lookin' like a movie star with those big sun glasses on."

"Girl, I need these shades to hide my blood shot eyes."

"You must have gone out last night."

"Yep. I went to a strip club down on Bourbon Street with Angela and Lisa."

"Why are you still hangin' with those hussies?"

"Well, I can't hang with my favorite Jezebel anymore—you," Lawana replied with much attitude. "You can't stay out past ten o'clock anymore."

"Whatever! How did y'all end up in a strip club, of all places?"

"I thought we were going to see some male strippers. Those heifers tricked me. Before the night was over I ended up in one of the back rooms getting a lap dance—from a woman."

"What? What happened to the men?"

"Girl, you know how wild those clubs are down in the French Quarters. No, I take that back. You wouldn't know how wild they are because Terry's possessive ass doesn't let you go anywhere or do anything."

"You sound jealous."

"Shiiit, I can never be jealous about the fact that you're on lock down and I'm not. If you like it, then that's a *you* issue."

Carmen didn't reply to her friend's snide remark. She held up her middle finger and continued to sip her coffee.

Lawana continued, "Anyway! The strip club we went to had male and female strippers. The three of us made a bet that the first one who got hit on by a woman would have to get a lap dance from a female stripper.

"I don't have to tell you who lost the damn bet. You know I'm strictly dickly; so I had to work up the courage to let a chick shake her ass in my face. I started ordering Long Island Iced Teas two at a time. I guess I had one too many because before I knew it, I was sitting on a couch in the backroom with some freak named Juicy straddling me. She had her tits all up in my face."

Carmen smiled. "You know you liked it."

"Giiiirl, that shit scared me."

"Why?"

Lawana took off her glasses and looked around the diner to make sure no one was eavesdropping on their conversation. She leaned over and whispered, "I got scared because I started to get turned on."

Carmen smiled again. "Ummm hmm, I knew your ass was bi-curious. You know I'm your girl; you can come out of the closet. I won't tell anyone."

"Bitch please! I started sobering up when Juicy smacked me across the face with those big bazookas."

"She did what?"

"You heard me. At first she was just straddling me and dancing. All of a sudden she grabbed those monster tits and then parted them like the Red Sea. Before I figured out what was going on she clapped my face with 'em."

Carmen nearly choked on her coffee. "What do you mean she clapped your face?"

"Did I stutter? I said she clapped my damn face. Instead of using her hands to smash my face, she grabbed her tits, spread them open, and then smashed my face in between them."

"What did you do?"

"I didn't do anything. I think I was in shock. I know one thing—that blew my high. She did it so hard my damn ears started ringing."

"So you just sat there?"

"I sat there until she tried some real freaky shit."

"What did she do?"

"Giiirl, I don't know how much money I gave that stripper, but she had a thick ass wad of cash in the waistband of her thong. At first she was straddling me and rolling her hips, and then she put her feet on each side of my chair and stood up over me. She actually tried to put her cat in my face."

"You're lying?"

"I wish I was, but I'm not."

Carmen's smirk turned into a chuckle when she saw the scared look on Lawana's face. "What did you do?"

"Cee, I just started reaching for my purse and screaming. I pushed that heifer off of me and ran out of there."

"No you didn't?"

"Bitch, do I look like I'm joking? I pushed her ass off of me and ran out of that room."

"You started running?"

"Running!"

"Actually running?"

"Like white women chasing a skinny nigga bouncing a basketball. Girl, I rushed straight out of that door and headed towards Canal Street to go get my car."

"Where were Angela and Lisa?"

"Girl, they were sitting at the table laughing their asses off, when they saw how I looked running past them. For all I know they're probably still sitting there laughing at me."

Carmen and Lawana giggled for a few seconds. Most of their encounters begin with Lawana telling some outlandish story, but this day as Carmen's light hearted laughter soon gave way to a gush of tears. She'd been trying to hold back her emotions since she first sat down.

"Damn, Cee. What's wrong?" asked Lawana, as she grabbed some napkins from the dispenser on their table and started wiping her friend's cheeks.

It took Carmen a few moments to regain her composure. When she was finally able to speak without crying, she told Lawana about the events from the night before.

"Lawana, I don't know what I'm gonna do."

"What happened? Did you and Terry get into another argument?"

"Yeah, but it's worse than that. QJ saw Quincy."

"What?"

"QJ saw his daddy."

"Where?"

"I don't know—somewhere around Claiborne Avenue He said Quincy is homeless. Somehow, the two of them met up."

"Oh shit!" Lawana replied, and then put her hand over her mouth in astonishment.

"That's all you have to say is, *Oh shit!* It was your recommendation that I tell the boy his daddy was dead in the first place. Now the only thing you can say is, *Oh Shit!*"

"Wait a minute. I simply made a suggestion," Lawana replied defensively. "You chose to go with that story. Hell, I've made several suggestions to you about your life—you didn't follow all of them. I told you to leave Terry's overbearing ass a long time ago, but you didn't listen to that suggestion."

"Well I followed your recommendation on this matter, and now the boy has met his father. I don't know what to do."

The two of them sat silently at the table for a few seconds. Carmen wiped her tears while Lawana sat there trying to think of a good suggestion.

"Cee, I'm sorry. I didn't think this would happen. When you and Quincy broke up, I didn't think you would ever see him again. Shit, he left you and didn't look back. He hasn't tried to help you support QJ emotionally or financially for ten years. For all intents and purposes he was dead."

Carmen didn't respond. She just nodded her head in agreement and stared at her coffee mug. The steam that once lingered above the cup like a morning fog was gone.

"How is QJ handling it?"

"He's furious. He came home last night pissed off. He looked like he wanted to choke the shit out of me. Girl, it was the first time I was actually scared of my own child."

"Poor baby," Lawana whispered. "I know he must have been devastated. Now that the truth is out you're gonna have to sit him down and try to explain everything that went down back when he was a child."

"I tried to talk to him last night, but he wasn't tryin' to hear me."

"I'm not surprised, Cee. You're gonna have to give him some time to digest this. He just found out that his father, whom he thought was dead, is alive and living right here in the same city with him."

"What if he decides he wants a relationship with Quincy?"

"You should tell him no!" Lawana shouted.

"Lawana, I can't stop him from seeing his daddy."

"Whatever! Quincy stopped being a *daddy* the day he walked away from his son. He's just a damn sperm donor as far as I'm concerned. I don't care what went on between you and him; he shouldn't have avoided his responsibilities."

"That may be true Lawana, but I made up this elaborate story about the man being dead. QJ is just as mad at me as he is with Quincy."

"You told him his daddy was dead because it was easier than telling him the truth! You can't beat yourself up for that. As far as I'm concerned, Quincy brought this on himself. He put you in a bad position."

"I shouldn't have lied."

"Whatever. I don't think you did anything wrong. When was the last time you heard from Quincy?"

"I don't know. Do you remember I told you that I thought I saw him standing outside the school after QJ's graduation from Elementary School?"

"Yeah, I remember you said you saw some grungy looking man who resembled him."

"Well, that must have been him."

"Look Cee, you've had to take care of that boy by yourself for all these years. Hell, I've been more of a father to him than Quincy. If he was still roaming around New Orleans he could have tried to provide some type of support for that child."

"Not if he's homeless."

"So! That's *his* problem."

"Not totally. I can't help but feel like I drove him to that lifestyle."

"Girl, please, I don't care what you did to hurt him. It's not your fault he turned to drugs and liquor for support. He chose that. He also chose not to provide financial support for his son. Any man that doesn't take care of his child shouldn't be allowed to see the child... period! You need to keep QJ away from him."

"QJ was already having a hard time accepting Terry. Now that Quincy is back in the picture, getting QJ to accept Terry is going to be impossible," said Carmen as tears streamed down her face.

"Does Terry know you lied about Quincy's death?"

"No."

"Good. Let's keep this between us until we can figure out what you should do next. Do you want me to come over and speak to my godson?"

"I guess… shit, I don't know. I honestly don't know what to do. I really messed this one up Lawana. I've messed up big time."

Chapter 4

Decrepit swings dangled helplessly from three different sets of swings. In the far corner of the neighborhood playground stood a rusty chain link backstop. The odd shaped monstrosity was located approximately sixty feet away from the remnants of a pitchers mound that now looked like an ant mound.

This playground was once a bastion of joy, hope, and inspiration. But, as in the case of most inner cities, when the city's parks and recreation budget shriveled up, so did the hopes and dreams of little boys and girls in the community.

Unkempt grass was now the norm. The stench of urine saturated the air. Fourteen year old girls searching for any form of attention from a man, could be seen getting fondled and hemmed up by men six and seven years older than them. Used syringes littered the grass along side brown paper bags that hugged empty Mad Dog 20/20 bottles.

During the day time, grown men still living out their hoop dreams could be seen playing pick up basketball games on a concrete slab with bare iron rims perched on top of crooked poles. At night, some of those same ballers could be seen peering from behind oak trees while they received blowjobs from the neighborhood crack fiends—men and women.

A playground like this would seem to be the last place on earth for a lost soul to find solace, but it was the one place where QJ knew he could go to clear his thoughts. Besides, it was nine o'clock on a Saturday morning; the playground was the quietest place within a two mile radius.

The drug dealers scurried from the bright morning sunlight like roaches when the lights come on. Crack heads were recovering from their drug induced slumbers.

The playground was QJ's sanctuary, and he intended to meditate there while he sorted through his dysfunctional home situation. Based on the plethora of thoughts bouncing around inside of his head at a frenetic pace, sorting things out would take a while.

I can't believe my mama has been lying to me for all of these years. How could she do that to me? Instead of allowing me to connect with him, she'd rather bring Terry's disgusting ass into my world. She can keep tryin', but I'm never gonna accept Terry.

I'm always hangin' out under that bridge with my crew – I wonder if he's been there all this time. I wonder if he's been watching me all this time. I can't believe I was about to beat him with that pipe.

I wonder why he never tried to contact me all of these years. Maybe he did try to reach out to me and my mama wouldn't let him talk to me. Yeah, that's probably how it went down; she was hatin' on him.

How could he let himself become homeless? Man that nigga must be lazy or somethin'. He could get a job at a car wash or some place – he doesn't have to be homeless unless he wanna be like that – livin' out of a damn shopping cart. The more I think about it, I'm kinda glad his deadbeat ass didn't holla at me all these years. I don't want anybody knowing he's my daddy.

Oh shit... Tweety and Bookie may already know. They were walkin' away so maybe they didn't hear him call my name. With all that noise out there that day, maybe they didn't hear him talk about my mama. But what if they did hear him? Shit! If dem niggas heard him call my name, and say that he was my daddy, they are gonna rib me for weeks. Damn, this is fucked up!

Later on that day, QJ went over to Bookie's house in the Lafitte projects. Like most housing projects in New Orleans, the Lafitte projects appeared relatively tame during the daytime. People were cordial but cautious. Outsiders were spotted, scrutinized, and even followed. Even though it was safe to wander around in the daytime hours, it was not a place where an outsider would want to be caught loitering after the sun went down.

QJ visited Bookie in the projects often. He'd been enough times by the residents to no longer be considered a threat – in essence he'd been issued a "ghetto pass". He knocked on Bookie's front door and was greeted by his friend's elderly grandmother – the boy's guardian.

"Bookie!" the woman shouted. "Come down here and talk to one of your little hoodlum friends!"

Bookie came down stairs wearing a pair of baggy shorts that hung so low they looked like a pair of long pants. He had a huge band-aid over his left eye.

"Wuz up, dog?" Bookie asked as he greeted QJ at the door.

"You need to either go outside or come inside," his grandmother shouted. "You lettin' out all of my cold air."

Bookie rolled his eyes at his grandmother and stepped outside. "Man, lets go outside – she's trippin'."

The two of them sat on the steps and talked.

"What's up, dog?" QJ asked. "How is your eye doing?"

"I'm cool," Bookie replied, and turned his head – clearly embarrassed by the bandage job his grandmother whipped up. "I'm just chillin'. What happened to you yesterday? Did the police catch you?"

"Nawh, I got away," QJ replied, curiously waiting for Bookie to say something that indicated he'd heard Quincy's comments.

"Where did you go? Me and Tweety didn't stop runnin' until we made it here."

"I ran into the Iberville."

"Man, that shit was crazy. That homeless dude snuck me. That's how he caught me off guard."

QJ expected Bookie to tweak the sequence of events so it wouldn't appear that he got whipped in a straight up fight. Truth be told, he didn't care how Bookie modified his story. They were a few minutes into their conversation, and Bookie still hadn't mentioned anything about Quincy's remarks. His secret was still safe.

"So, what y'all gettin' into today?" QJ asked.

"Nothin' for now," Bookie replied. "Later on tonight we are goin' back to deal with that bum."

"What?"

"C'mon, dog. You know I can't go out like this. That fool split my eye and got me walkin' around here lookin' like a mummy. I gotta get him back for that."

QJ's heart rate sped up. He knew Bookie was serious. Bookie's ego wouldn't allow the word to get out in the 'hood that he'd been beaten up by a homeless man. His reputation would be shot—ass whippings from neighborhood thugs would become the norm. Retaliation was not only inevitable, it was mandated.

"Man, you should just leave that shit alone."

Bookie looked at QJ with annoyance. "Nigga, you must be crazy if you think I'm just gonna let that fool get away with this. That fool gotta get dealt with. Are you rollin' with us?"

QJ knew backing out at this point would damage his own reputation. He mulled over his rowdy friend's comment before he replied.

"What time y'all gonna go and get him?"

"We're gonna wait until around 8 o'clock tonight. I wanna wait until it gets dark. My brother showed me how to make a shank when he got out of jail. I made a nice one last week. I've been waiting to use this thing, and now I have my chance."

Retaliation was nothing new to QJ, but participating in the possible murder of his own father was a scenario he was having a hard time embracing. He had to think fast – real fast.

"Yeah, I'm down for that. I'm gonna come back over here around 7 o'clock," he said and then gave his friend some dap.

"Cool. I thought you were about to punk out on me," said Bookie.

"Nawh, I'm down for a little pay back," QJ replied nervously. "I'll see you later tonight."

QJ left his friend sitting on those project steps. His walk back to his house was long and intense. He played the scene out in his head.

Damn, they're gonna fuck him up if they catch him. I should let them do it – it ain't like I know him. I don't owe him anything. Why should I look out for him? He hasn't looked out for me, or my mama during the past ten years.

Quincy spent hours in the Emergency Room after the beating he'd suffered. His head was bandaged. His eye was swollen. His thick lips were even puffier than usual. They actually hid the open space created by the missing tooth. His ribs were bruised and his attempts to block the blows with his hands left his right wrist swollen. Lack of healthcare meant he'd have to nurse himself back to health. No dental coverage ensured he'd have to forego any modeling opportunities requiring him to smile.

Prior to the assault, Quincy always looked like he was just a shower and shave away from being able to blend back in with the working class. After the beating he'd taken, his physical appearance mirrored his mental and emotional state.

Rather than leave the comfort of the hospital and deal with the inclement weather that had roared through the city during the midnight hour, he found a quiet spot in a corner to rest his head. The lone security guard on duty felt sorry for him and allowed him to rest uninterrupted.

It was nearly noon the next day when Quincy finally made his way back to the site of his beat down. Ironically, the physical beating he took didn't hurt as much as the fact that when he finally returned to his spot under the bridge, half of the contents in his shopping cart had been pilfered by his homeless brethren.

His cardboard box, which he'd spent several hours tailoring to his dimensions so it could serve as both shelter and a bed, was gone. His can opener was gone. A new roll of duct tape—gone. His chipped butter knife—gone. His fork with the crooked prongs—gone. His dingy spoon—gone. The plate he used to hold the half eaten meals he procured from fast food restaurant tables—gone.

Losing those items was bothersome, but the thing that made him sick to his stomach was the absence of a wool blanket he'd had since his childhood. That blanket was his most prized possession. It was irreplaceable. The absence of that blanket brought tears to his eyes that weren't present even while he was being beaten.

Quincy wiped his eyes and sat down on the ground at the base of one of the huge columns. He tried to figure out his next move, but eventually his thoughts strayed.

My boy has gotten so big. He looks just like me. I wonder if he was able to get away. Those cops chasing him looked determined to catch him. If he ran in the direction I told him to he should have escaped.

He said his mother told him I was dead. Why would she do that? I know she probably hates me for leaving, but she didn't have to tell the boy I was dead. I can tell from the look in his eyes that he didn't want to hurt me. He's not a bad kid. Well, he's not as vicious as those other boys he's hangin' with.

I wonder if he could tell that I miss him. I wonder if he could tell that I still love him. I wonder if I will ever see him again.

Quincy's pensive moment was interrupted by his neighbor's voice.

"Are you okay?" asked the old lady who'd tried to discourage the attack.

"Yeah, I'm okay," Quincy replied.

"You don't look okay. Are you hungry? I have some leftover chicken from a meal I had earlier. You are welcome to a piece."

Quincy's stomach was in knots from hunger pains. He didn't want to take her up on her offer, but his body was demanding he take her up on her offer.

He tore into that chicken like a hungry pit bull. His mouth was sore and the missing tooth made it hard to enjoy the meat, but his hunger trumped any discomfort.

"You know, I see those boys around here all the time. They will probably come back soon. You should think about relocating," said the wise old lady.

Quincy didn't reply. He kept his head down and focused on his meal.

"You know she's right. You should get out of here," said a male voice.

Quincy stopped gnawing on the chicken bone long enough to look up. He was shocked to see the voice belonged to one of his attackers—QJ.

A rush of emotions overtook Quincy. He was once again face-to-face with his only child. Visions of the doctor turning to him and asking him if he wanted to cut the umbilical cord flashed across his mind. The little baby who was six pounds - five ounces at birth, was now close to six feet tall and looking down at him as he sat on the ground looking helpless.

Quincy quickly stood up. He wasn't sure if QJ was preparing to attack or if he'd come in peace. QJ's next comment let Quincy know it was the latter.

"I know some place you can go where they won't find you," QJ said.

"I'm not runnin' from them," Quincy replied defiantly.

QJ looked surprised. A frown came across his face. He took a step back and immediately began to regret his decision to try and save his father's life.

"Fine. Stay yo ass here. I'm tryin' to help you stay alive. I know one thing, if you're here tonight, you probably won't live to see tomorrow."

QJ looked at his father from head to toe, shook his head in disgust, and turned to walk away. That was his first and last attempt to intervene. He could now take solace in the fact that he'd at least tried to save his father from Bookie's wrath.

"Wait, son!" Quincy shouted.

Quincy's words caused QJ to stop in his tracks. Despite the circumstances surrounding their reunion and the level of awkwardness that resonated through their discourse, something inside of QJ forced him to acquiesce to his father's commands.

"Where do you think I should go?"

QJ turned around slowly. He was still confused and angry about his father's absence from his life, but considering he helped him escape the law the day before, QJ felt he owed Quincy.

"You should move to the other end of Claiborne. Go to Palmer Park. It's on the corner of Claiborne Avenue and Carrollton Avenue in the 17th ward around Hollygrove and Pigeon Town. They have a lot of enemies around there so I know they won't search for you over there."

"That's way on the other end of Claiborne Avenue. Shit, that's gotta be 15 to 20 miles away," Quincy replied.

"It's kind of far, but like I said, they ain't tryin' to go over there," QJ replied.

QJ reached into his pocket and pulled out some cash. "Here's about ten dollars, you can use this money to catch the Claiborne bus. Across the street from the park is a grocery store, you can pick up another shopping cart from the parking lot."

QJ extended his hand to give Quincy the cash. The mixture of anger, hurt, and love caused the boy's hand to shake uncontrollably. Sensing his son's emotional state, Quincy grabbed the money and attempted to put his hand on QJ's shoulder. His attempt at affection was rebuffed. QJ flinched and moved away. It was clear that his emotional fences would take longer to mend than the wounds on Quincy's face.

"Man, just take the money," QJ said.

"Will I see you again?" Quincy asked.

QJ didn't reply. He turned and walked away without looking back. Quincy's heart sank. The chicken he'd just eaten was fighting to make its way from the pit of his stomach and back up through his throat.

As he watched QJ walk away he could feel the tears that had subsided return. He sat back on the ground up against the column and allowed his head to bow. Defeated he looked. Ashamed he felt.

"That child loves you," said the old lady.

Quincy looked at the woman through tear filled eyes as she retreated inside of her cardboard home. Quincy could no longer see her body, but he could still see her face.

"I don't know what happened in the past, but I can tell that God sent that child back into your life," said the woman. "Take it from an old lady with a lot of regrets; you can't let this opportunity pass. When he comes back you need to grab hold of him and never let him go."

Unlike his pubescent son, Quincy was able to identify one of God's angels; therefore, when the old woman spoke to him he listened intently.

"You think he'll come back?"

The woman winked at Quincy and unleashed an angelic grin just before she vanished completely into the darkness of her cave.

"Oh trust me honey, he'll be back. He needs his daddy… he'll be back."

QJ did come back, but he wasn't alone. Darkness dominated as Bookie, Tweety, and QJ walked amongst the bums in Tent City. They snaked past the homeless like a pack of Grim Reapers searching to issue some unlucky soul his ticket to hell.

QJ didn't want to be there, but he knew his reputation was on the line. He went along with Bookie's plot secretly hoping that Quincy had taken heed to his warning.

"He was right in this area!" whispered Bookie, trying not to alert anyone of their presence.

"I know," replied Tweety, as he yanked the flimsy flap of one of the tents.

Tweety found an elderly man coiled up like a snake inside. The man looked terrified.

"Close my door!" he shouted.

"Shut up, old man!" said Tweety and then ripped the entire flap off. The cheap material tore at the seams like wet paper.

"I don't see him," Quincy said, pretending he was actually looking.

"Hey old lady," said Bookie, speaking to the elderly woman that tried her hardest to thwart their attack on Quincy. "Where is that bum?"

"Who?" asked the woman, clearly frightened by the boy's harsh tone.

"Don't play dumb. You know who I'm talkin' about. You were tryin' to save him yesterday. Don't try to pretend like you don't know who I'm talkin' about."

"Child, I don't know nothin' 'bout what you're talkin' 'bout. Y'all kids need to go home."

"What?" asked Bookie, as he readied to smack the woman for questioning their presence. "I should…"

"Leave her alone," said QJ.

"What?"

"You heard me. Leave her alone!" said QJ once again. "We didn't come here for her. You're always gettin' distracted. That old woman ain't worth our time. Let's just go and come back another time. We can catch that fool when he least expect it. He gonna come back here one day thinkin' we forgot about him. We can deal with him when we run into him again."

"I agree. We'll get him when we run into him again," said Tweety. "I'm hungry. Let's go get somethin' to eat."

Bookie didn't appreciate QJ interfering, but once Tweety sided with QJ, Bookie knew he had no choice but to go along with their suggestion.

Bookie looked at the woman and then spat in her direction. QJ shoved him out of the way and then looked back at the woman. Before he could turn and walk away, the lady gestured for him to bend down to her level.

When Bookie was too far away to hear their conversation, QJ kneeled down and pretended to be tying his shoe laces.

"Lady, I just saved your life. What do you want?"

"Your daddy left earlier. He went to that park you told him about," the lady whispered.

QJ nodded and then stood up. He let out a silent sigh of relief once he knew that his father had taken his advice. Quincy was safe, and QJ's clout with his buddies remained in tact.

Quincy relocated to Palmer Park like his son instructed. Palmer Park was quiet. It was a popular spot for white yuppies walking their dogs and speed walkers looking to shed a few pounds. Because of its location on the corner of Carrollton Avenue and Claiborne Avenue, the park was void of much of the seediness that accompanied many of the playgrounds in the city.

Quincy searched for a quiet corner to set up camp. After noticing a bench located in the far corner of the park near a huge Magnolia tree, he headed that way. Exhausted and eager to take a nap, Quincy plopped down on the bench.

"Not there," said a voice from the bushes.

The unfamiliar voice startled Quincy. He quickly turned around to see the owner, and was surprised to see it was a guy he'd attended high school with.

"Scoop, is that you?" Quincy asked, immediately recognizing the tall lanky man.

Sedrick "Scoop" Bowe was a high school basketball star in the early eighties. He was courted by numerous colleges, eventually committing to Southern University in Baton Rouge. Unfortunately, Scoops inability to read caught up with him. After two semesters, he was placed on academic probation and eventually lost his scholarship.

Quincy and Scoop weren't the best of friends, but were always cordial to each other. They'd even dated the same girl at one time; a fact that came to light one day in the gymnasium when they both approached her from different directions looking for a hug.

Quincy was more handsome and a better dresser than Scoop, but Scoop's promising athletic career and popularity gave him the upper hand in the *skirt chasing* arena.

Nevertheless, Quincy and Scoop remained casual acquaintances. They hadn't seen each other in nearly twenty years. Neither would have predicted that their paths would cross again twenty years later while jockeying for position in a park.

"Yeah, I'm Scoop. Who are you?"

"It's me, Quincy Washington from high school."

Scoop was just coming off of his heroin-induced high so it took a moment for him to remember Quincy. Eventually, his memory caught up with the moment.

"Quincy Washington? Not Quincy Washington from Fortier High School?"

"Yeah, bruh."

"The same Quincy Washington that tried to steal my woman?" Scoop asked, chuckling as he extended his hand to give Quincy some dap.

"Well, that ain't how I remember it, but if that's how you wanna put it," Quincy replied, and gave Scoop some dap.

"Man, I ain't seen yo ass in nearly twenty years. Where you been?"

"I've been around," Quincy replied, overcome with a sudden rush of embarrassment.

Scoop saw the look on Quincy's face. "Aw, man. It's all good. We're in the same boat. You ain't gotta worry about me judgin' you."

Scoop pointed to a nearby tree. "That spot right there is vacant."

"Is this spot taken?" Quincy asked, preferring to stay where he was.

"Yeah, this is my spot. As a matter of fact, you're standing in my living room right now," Scoop replied, and let out a hearty laugh. "You gotta excuse the place. I'm redecorating at the moment."

The two men sat on the bench. The stench of their sweat drenched bodies combined to create an odor that would have chased a skunk away.

"So, what brings you to this neck of the woods?" Scoop asked. "I've been hangin' out here for a year. I've never seen you around here."

"I had been hangin' out around Canal Street. I got into a little beef so I figured I should find a quieter spot."

"Well, you found the right spot. This place is quiet. Nobody botherin' you. No police harassing you. You don't have to worry about fools tryin' to steal your shit. I like it here."

Quincy stared at Scoop. When he last saw Scoop he was on the front page of the Times Picayune Sports section holding the high school state championship basketball trophy. The dude was a playground legend. Everyone thought he was destined for the NBA.

Scoop was used to getting that same look from people he went to high school with. He was a tragic tale of a dream deferred. When Jay-Z said in his song, *Izzo (H.O.V.A.)*, "I've seen hoop dreams deflate, like a true fiends weight", he was talking about the Scoop Bowe's of the world.

"Yeah, I know you're wonderin' how I ended up like this," Scoop said, opting to cut to the chase rather than spend any more time avoiding discussing the pink elephant sitting on the bench along side them.

Quincy continued to stare at Scoop. No response was necessary. The blank look on his face spoke volumes.

Scoop rolled up his right sleeve. Needle marks covered his entire forearm and elbow area. At first glance it looked like he had a rash or freckles, but the infected areas surrounding his vein told the true story.

"Yeah, I fucked up," Scoop said in a melancholy tone. "I flunked out of school and had to come back home. I was depressed, and rather than working on getting myself together, I got distracted by drugs. Weed lead to crack. Crack lead to heroin. The rest is history."

Quincy was still staring at Scoop while he talked. He thought his alcoholism had him down and out, but Scoop was definitely in a worse position.

"So, that's my story in a nutshell. What's yours?"

Quincy turned and looked away. He didn't really want to swap horror stories, but he knew he had to. It was an unwritten rule. If someone shares their story and you don't stop them, you are required to share yours. It was expected. Some unwritten rules are more important than the written ones.

True to form, Quincy rubbed his hand across his mouth and cheek; a tell-tale sign that he was uncomfortable with a situation. He looked at Scoop and then down at his old classmate's arm.

"C'mon, bruh. Give it up. Ma'fucka's don't just wake up one morning and say, "I think I wanna be homeless." Nawh, we both know the shit doesn't work like that. Everybody out here got a story. Some cats are on drugs. Some are just fucked up in the head mentally. Some just fell on hard times; hell, I met a white boy last week in City Park—right across the street from Tulane University. That ma'fucka used to be a damn economics professor at Tulane."

"How did he end up on the streets?"

"Man the shit is crazy. He told me his wife left him. She ran off with one of his former students. On top of that, she cleaned out their bank account—left that ma'fucka broke as a joke."

"That's some cold shit," Quincy said.

"Tell me about it. She took the dog and everything. I think that fucked him up more than her leaving. You know how white folk are about their pets; some of them treat their dogs better than they treat other humans."

"True that," Quincy added.

"Anyway, this white boy had just built his woman a big-ass house in the Garden District. Ma'fucka said he was so depressed after everything happened; he just walked away from it all. The house. The car. The bills. Everything. He even quit his job; said he couldn't teach anymore because too many of the students knew what happened.

"It's easy to assume everybody out here that's homeless are just crazy, but that ain't always the case. Everybody has a story; so, I'm gonna ask you again… what's yours?"

Quincy sighed loudly. "I never thought I'd end up like this."

"None of us do," Scoop interjected.

"Man, my life was going smoothly. I had a good job. No I had a good *career*."

"What were you doing for a living?" Scoop asked. "If I recall correctly, you were always kind of smart and shit."

"After high school I went to Nicholls State. I got a degree in Accounting. After college I started working at City Hall. I was making good money. I got married when I was 22 years old."

"First mistake," Scoop said. "Brothas who get married that young usually regret it. There are too many women out here to be getting tied down that young. You gotta get out and have some fun first. If not, you spend the rest of your life wishing you had partied more. That shit's a recipe for a disaster."

"Have you ever been married?"

"Hell no! Back in the day I was too busy gettin' my pimp on to be marrying anybody."

"Well, I did tie the knot when I was younger, and everything was cool—for awhile."

"Hmm," Scoop uttered sarcastically, feeling like Quincy's acknowledgment that things were only cool for a short time only confirmed his theory about men getting married too soon. "Let me guess, she caught you tipping around with some other chick."

"Nope. It was actually the other way around."

Scoop looked at Quincy and shook his head. "My theory applies to women too. Getting married before the age of thirty is a mistake."

"So, what's your poison?" Scoop asked.

"At first it was liquor. Yeah, Hennessey was my thing. I used to drink that shit like it was Kool-Aid. When we were in high school I didn't smoke or drink, but once I got married and the problems at home started, I started sippin' on that damn Hennessey."

"Damn, dog. That Hennessey is some expensive shit. How'd you start out with that?" asked Scoop, as he pulled out a wrinkled cigarette pack and removed two crooked cigarettes — passing one to Quincy.

Scoop lit both of their cigarettes and they both took long drags in unison. It was Quincy's first cigarette in a week. He closed his eyes and savored the menthol taste before continuing.

"I told you, I had a good job. I could afford it. The problem is, the more I drank that shit, the worse my attendance record at work got."

"What made you take it to the next level?"

"I caught my wife in some shit," Quincy replied, as he took another long puff. "Man, what she did totally fucked with my head. Eventually I just had to get away from it all. That's when I started using that dope harder."

"I feel you," Scoop replied, with an empathetic look. "You got any kids?"

The question sent chills down Quincy's spine. He found himself in that odd space where absentee fathers dwell. It was like he was in parental purgatory. His paternal instincts wanted him to openly profess to be a proud father, but his conscious held his words in check. His manhood had been snatched from him by his own absenteeism; rendering him emotionally castrated — emasculated like a eunuch.

"Uhhh, yeah," Quincy hesitantly replied. "I got a little boy. He's fifteen."

Scoop may have been a junkie, but he was wise beyond his years. He could see the conversation had taken a turn down a road Quincy clearly wasn't prepared to travel.

"Look bruh, kids have a way of looking past our faults. Take some time to get your thoughts together and then go get right with your son. I assume that's what you want, right?"

Quincy could no longer hold his head high. Tear drops could be seen splashing on his dirty pant legs. Scoop knew when to pull up. He placed his hand on Quincy's shoulder as a sign of support.

"This is only a temporary state. For what it's worth, there is a dude that always comes around here once a week, offerin' to help us get cleaned up."

Quincy wiped his tears and looked at Scoop. "Why haven't you taken him up on his offer?"

Scoop took one last puff of his cigarette and then threw it in the grass. He let the smoke shoot from his mouth and nostrils, and stared at the toxic cloud for a few seconds before it dissipated.

"I'm a lost cause. My mama died five years ago. I never knew my daddy—the nigga was a deadbeat. I don't have any kids, but I gotta admit, sometimes I do wish I had at least one child."

"Why? Do you think it would have changed the outcome of your life?"

"I don't know. Maybe. Maybe not. I kinda feel the way Tupac described in one of his songs. I forget which song it was, but it's the one when he says, 'Lately, I've been really wantin' babies, so I can see a part of me that wasn't always shady.'"

"Yeah, I remember that line," Quincy replied.

Scoop continued. "I'm an only child so I never had any siblings to give me any nephews or nieces. Bottom line, I don't have any reason to get cleaned up… but it sounds like you do."

The two homeless men sat silently on the bench for the next five minutes. Scoop was pondering his next move while Quincy sat there reflecting on Scoop's wise words.

"Look man, I'm hungry. I'm about to go and score me a rock and then go across the street and get somethin' to eat. You want me to get you somethin'?"

Quincy secretly desired to follow Scoop to the dope spot. He didn't have any money, but the crack head in him figured he could at least bum a puff or two.

"You got that look in your eyes, playboy," Scoop said. "I'ma be straight up with you dog, I ain't big on sharing my shit."

Quincy knew he didn't have the resources to return the favor so he didn't comment further. He'd gone two weeks without smoking crack. It was a struggle at times, but he was trying his hardest to quit.

There are all types of addictions: drugs, gambling, alcohol, cigarettes, and others. Quincy learned a long time ago that it doesn't make sense for a person to have an addiction he couldn't afford. Addictions are fed off of two things: desire and money. If you kill the desire, you don't have to worry about the money. Quincy never fully killed his desire for crack cocaine, but his lack of cash did help squelch the desire somewhat.

Now that his crack itch was lying dormant he fought like hell to keep it subdued. To partake again after such a long hiatus would only force him to look for ways to support his habit. Homeless and addicted he may have been, but a robber or thief he wasn't. On the other hand, a pint of Thunderbird was within his price range. Sipping on cheap wine was his forced vice of choice.

Scoop looked as if he was going to walk towards the nearby playground, and then stopped and changed directions.

"Where are you going?" Quincy asked.

"I changed my mind," Scoop replied, as he stood there staring across the street at the grocery store. "I'm gonna go ahead and go to the grocery store across the street. I got the hookup, but I need to catch her before she leaves."

"Who is she—a relative?"

"Back in the day I used to date the chick who now runs the sandwich department. She be hookin' a nigga up. She only works on weekdays—I gotta catch her early because once she gets busy it's hard for her to get to me."

"Are you going inside?"

"Nawh, she meets me behind the store everyday around this time. She be givin' a nigga all kinds of sandwiches and shit. She even be puttin' toothpaste and soap and shit in the bag. I'ma take care of you, but you gonna have to get your own shopping cart from the parking lot."

"I hear you," Quincy replied, and then stood up.

"The best time to get a shopping cart is in the afternoon between three and five. They usually don't have a security guard in the parking lot during that time frame. It's usually easy, people who live around here and walk to the store are always pushing the shopping carts to the edge of the parking lot before they remove the stuff they bought and carry it to their house. All you gotta do is grab one of those carts they leave at the edge of the lot."

Scoop grabbed the lapel of his overcoat and pulled it tighter. He acted like he was walking in some Northeast city during middle of winter. He boldly held up his hand as he crossed the three lane avenue. Cars came to a sudden stop as they waited for the cocky vagabond to strut past.

Quincy was amused by the boldness Scoop displayed. He acted like he owned the streets. Like he was the reigning king of that neighborhood, and anyone passing by should pay homage.

Quincy turned and looked around at his new home. It was time to get settled in now that he'd received his crash course on how to be a vagrant in Palmer Park. Courtesy of a one time basketball star affectionately called Scoop.

Chapter 5

"Ma'am, these jeans have been worn already. I can't let you return them," Carmen stated to the angry woman standing on the other side of the counter.

"Bullshit!" shouted the skinny white woman. "Y'all gonna give me my damn money back. I told you I never wore those jeans."

"Ma'am, there is a red stain on the leg of these jeans and dirt stains on the seat of the jeans," Carmen replied, as she held up the jeans to show the customer.

"I don't give a damn! I told you I've never worn these jeans. Those stains must have been there when I purchased them last week!"

Carmen wanted to bark back at the ignorant woman, but she knew she couldn't. The new General Manager of the store was a firm believer that the customer was always right. However, Carmen knew that she would be in trouble if she accepted the damaged merchandise. That same General Manager would reprimand her behind closed doors for allowing the transaction to take place.

As she stared at the irate customer, Carmen knew that arguing with her was a no-win proposition. *Stay professional, Carmen. Don't lose your cool.*

The customer stood there with her arms crossed and smacked on the gum that danced between her teeth and cheeks. The woman's bold stance caught Carmen off guard. This white girl had a lot of attitude.

Oh she's one of them. I guess she has a few black girlfriends or she's dating a black dude, so now she thinks she can handle a sista.

Carmen's anger level rose to an all-time high when she heard the woman's next comment.

"Look woman," said the customer, in full *sista girl* mode with her finger wagging and neck rolling. "You're gonna give me my damn money back or I'm gonna take it out of your ass!"

No this little skinny white bitch didn't just say she was gonna kick my ass. Looord, Jesus Christ, I need you now. Pleeeease keep me from choking this heifer.

The other two customers standing in line immediately took steps backwards. They weren't sure what was about to happen, but it was clear that they wanted to be far enough away to avoid any wild punches that were about to be thrown.

"Excuse me?" Carmen asked, totally caught off guard by the woman's comment.

"Bitch, you heard me!" replied the woman, as she sat her purse on the floor and started to remove her earrings. "I don't know what kind of white women you are used to dealin' with, but I'm from the 9th Ward, boo."

Did she just call me a bitch? Lord, I don't believe this is happening. This white woman wants to fight me. She just called me out in front of all of these people. I know this bitch, didn't just call me a bitch.

Carmen's inner voices were talking to her. The responsible voice was encouraging her to maintain her cool. But, that inner voice that was born and raised in the 9th ward was urging her to get ghetto.

Yep, she did just call you a bitch. What you gonna do? I know you ain't gonna let this stringy hair white girl call you out.

Carmen's hands begin to shake as the anger started to filter throughout her limbs. She started shifting from side to side like she had to urinate. While she silently stood there mulling over her options, the customer took things to another level.

She raised her index finger and pointed it within two inches of Carmen's nose.

Carmen's responsible inner voice kicked in to over-drive. *Carmen, you need this job. Kicking this woman's ass may make you feel good right now, but you will lose the only means of support you have for yourself and QJ. This skank ain't worth it. Bite your tongue, not this heifer's finger.*

"You got five seconds to give me my money back or I'm gonna snatch your black ass from behind that counter!"

Carmen had heard enough. Her 9th Ward voice won the battle.

Oh, hell no! If you don't grab this woman's neck and choke the shit outta of her, you ain't gon' ever be able to look yourself in the mirror again.

"You ain't gonna snatch a damn thing!" Carmen blurted out and flung the jeans in the woman's face. "What you're gonna do is take these dirty-ass jeans back and get the hell outta here!"

Before the customer could respond, the Store Manager walked up. He wasn't sure what had provoked the altercation, but the way the other customers started to scatter told him he needed to intervene.

"What seems to be the problem here?"

Suddenly, the incensed customer transformed right before Carmen's eyes. Her nostrils were no longer flaring. Her fists were no longer clinched. Her eyes were no longer filled with rage. In fact, they were filling with tears. This woman who was acting like a pit bull only seconds earlier had miraculously transformed into an innocent lamb.

"Are you the manager?" the woman asked.

"Yes, I am," he replied. "I'm Mr. Carter, the Store Manager. What seems to be the problem?"

"I came in here to return these jeans. Apparently, they were damaged when I purchased them last week, but I didn't notice it until I pulled them out of the bag this morning."

Mr. Carter examined the jeans. "Yeah, I can see the stains. You didn't notice this last week?"

The woman turned up her damsel in distress act. Somehow she managed to let a tear leak from her eye and made her bottom lip quiver.

"No I didn't. I am unemployed right now. I don't have money to waste. If I had seen those stains on those jeans I wouldn't have bought them. Whenever I can save up a little money to buy some clothes for myself or my kids, I always come here. But, I have never been treated like this. Your employee is giving me a hard time. All I want is my money back. This has really upset me. I'm going to write a letter to your corporate office."

Carmen interjected, "Mr. Carter, all I tried to do was…"

Carmen's attempt to defend her position was thwarted by the stop sign hand gesture Mr. Carter threw in her direction.

"Ma'am, here at Dillards we take pride in servicing our loyal customers. I apologize for the inconvenience. We will definitely return your money," said Mr. Carter.

He turned and looked in the direction of a nearby employee and signaled for the man to come over. "John, I need you to take care of this customer's return. Carmen, I need you to meet me in my office now."

As Carmen stepped away from the cash register, she glanced back at the woman. The lady wiped her fake tear, smirked, and rolled her eyes at Carmen.

Angry is too weak of a word to describe how Carmen felt at that moment. She was only trying to do her job, and now she was about to be reprimanded. She felt like a kid being summoned to the Principals office. As juvenile as it may seem, Carmen was tempted to close her fist, touch both of her eyes and mouth, and then point at the lady the way kids used to do when they were silently threatening to beat up another child after school or on the playground.

Mr. Carter was a card-carrying Uncle Tom. This was his first General Manager position, and he wasn't about to allow a complaint over a pair of jeans escalate to a level above him. Pacifying that customer, while humiliating Carmen in the process, was much easier than trying to explain the situation to his white superiors.

The meeting with Mr. Carter was short and sweet. He talked and she listened. Her attempts to justify her actions were futile. Carmen was reprimanded for arguing with the customer and not using better judgment. She was also informed that her recent application for a management level position would be tainted by the incident.

I'll be damned. All I tried to do was enforce the policy he's always harping on, and his punk ass just left me hanging. I should take off my heels and stab him in his frog eyes. There ain't no way in the world he would have allowed a sista to return those dirty ass pants. I have been a model employee for five years, and this is the way I get treated.

Carmen left work that day feeling disgraced. Despite her exemplary track record, which included several "Employee of the Month" honors, she'd just learned a harsh lesson about life in the workplace for minorities. All of her awards equated to the pats on the back we commonly refer to as, *atta boys*. That incident with the customer caused her and those around her to say, "awwh, shit." What's the life lesson she learned? She learned it only takes one *awwh shit* to wipe out a dozen, *atta boys*.

Unfortunately, Carmen's headaches didn't stop at the job. Little did she know, her home life was about to take a turn that was so drastic it would make that work incident seem trivial in comparison.

Nearly a week had passed since the truth about Quincy's existence had come to light. Carmen and QJ intentionally avoided each other. QJ was angry about his mother's dishonesty. Carmen was ashamed of her dishonesty. The tension in the house was building like the lava churning inside of a volcano. An eruption was inevitable; when and where it would happen were the only unknowns.

As she sat at her kitchen table and sipped coffee from her favorite mug, she started reflecting on all that was transpiring in her life.

My son hates me. He hasn't come out and said it to my face, but he doesn't have to – his actions are speaking loud and clear.

I can remember a time when he'd come home from school and hug me, kiss me, and joke with me – all before taking off his book bag. These days I barely get acknowledged. He just comes in here at all hours of the evening and heads straight to the kitchen to get a glass of kool-aid, some cookies, and then marches up the stairs to his bedroom. No hello. No interest in how my day went. No desire to talk about how his day went.

It's like we are strangers. Like I'm the manager at some cheap motel and he's some drifter passing through town trying to keep a low profile. The place he used to call home is now just a place where he can take a shower and lay his head.

I wish I could chalk his behavior up to some kind of teenage phase that all kids go through, but I know better than that. QJ's behavior has been getting progressively worse over the years. My decision to give Terry a key to the house just made things worse.

Just when I thought things couldn't get worse, QJ runs into Quincy. After all these years, Quincy decides to show up. Now I have to deal with this shit.

God, I know You won't place more on me than I can handle, but I'm gonna need you to cut a sista some slack. I can't take much more.

Carmen's pensive moment was interrupted by the loud ringing of her cordless phone. She looked at the name on the caller I.D.screen.

Citifinancial. Y'all can call all day, but I'm not gonna answer. I'll send the car payment when I get the money.

You see, that's what I mean God. You know what I'm dealin' with in my personal life. You know I'm already stressed out. Now these bill collectors are bugging me. No disrespect God, but this is some bullshit. I don't bother anyone. I mind my on business. I've been going to church. I've even started paying tithes. But You keep sending this drama my way.

Carmen took a sip of her coffee and then thought about that last thought. She wasn't sure if criticizing God's action qualified as blasphemy, but she knew she was walking a fine line. To be on the safe side, she tried to clean up her thoughts. The last thing she wanted to do was piss God off.

God, you know I don't mean any disrespect. I'm just struggling with all of this. I assume You are the one sending this drama my way. Maybe it's the devil sending the drama my way, and You are allowing him to test me. Shit, I don't know whose plan it was to shake up my world like this, all I know is I can't take much more.

What I need from You right now, God is some guidance on how to deal with my son. How do I explain what happened between me and his father? Was I wrong for telling him Quincy was dead? Would it have been better to tell the boy his daddy didn't want to be bothered? Now that the truth is out, what should I say?

The pastor at church said we are supposed to stand still and wait for guidance from You. Well God, that's what I'm gonna do. I'm just gonna avoid addressing this issue with QJ until You guide my words. If I try to talk to him now I'm just gonna make matters worse. Yeah, that's what I'm gonna do — wait on You.

Carmen paused and sipped again. Her tense facial expressions contradicted her desire to act and think positively.

But how will I know it's You talking to me? What if it's the devil trying to make things worse for me? What if the voice I hear isn't Yours God? Shit, I'm confused. My damn head is hurting. God forgive me, but this coffee ain't getting the job done right now. I need a glass of Chardonnay.

The doorbell chime startled Carmen. She rolled her eyes as she walked towards the door. The headache caused by the events of the day had soured her mood. Her feet ached and her body yearned for a good massage. Peeking through the peep hole, her frown turned to a smile when she saw Lawana standing outside.

"Girl, what are you doing here?" she asked.

"I told you I was going to come over and see my godson," Lawana replied, as she walked in and gave Carmen a hug. "You look worn out."

"Girl, I've been at that damn job for the past twelve hours. I need to rest," Carmen replied. "I got reprimanded today and on top of that, I'm so hungry I can eat a damn horse. A stiff drink wouldn't hurt."

"No, what you need is a stiff dick," Lawana replied.

"Girl, do you ever stop thinking about sex?"

"Nope. I'm gonna be seventy years old thinking about it. I'm gonna make sure I have a young man hangin' around to scratch my itch."

"You're gonna need somebody your own age to calm you down."

"Shiiit, you know I like 'em young. A man my age can't do nothing for me, but pay my bills."

"And what can a young man do?"

"All the shit a man my age is too tired to do like pick me up off of my feet, and sex me while standing up."

"You've been watching too many porn movies."

"I know. Those movies have made me raise my standards," Lawana replied proudly.

"You little freak," Carmen said, as she shook her head.

"That's Ms. Freak to you," Lawana replied flippantly. "Now, where is QJ? I'm gonna take him out for a few hours."

"He's upstairs in his room," Carmen responded. The hopelessness in her voice was all Lawana needed to hear to know that her visit was long overdue.

"Have the two of you talked about what happened?"

"No. Honestly, I don't have the energy to get into any discussions about Quincy."

Lawana turned and walked up the stairs towards QJ's bedroom. His bedroom door was partially open so Lawana barged in. QJ was sitting with his back to the door. He had a pair of headphones on while he played his Play Station.

Lawana snatched the headphones and playfully smacked QJ across his head. Lawana and QJ's relationship was special. She was the voice of reason in his world; the one person whom he never disrespected or talked back to.

"Hey, Lawana!" QJ said.

"What's up, boy?"

"Nothin… just chillin'."

"Have you eaten?"

"No. Why? Are you gonna take me to get somethin'?"

"Yeah, that's why I came over here. Put on your shoes so we can leave."

Quincy turned off his game and grabbed his tennis shoes.

"Oh, hell no!" Lawana barked. "You ain't followin' me lookin' like a little chain snatcher."

"Why'd you call me that?"

"You look like a little thug, QJ. I can see your underwear. You need to put a belt on or somethin', and take that ghetto-ass wave cap off of your head. I can't stand seeing boys walkin' around like that. You look like a clown. Y'all think that shit is cute. Ain't nothin' cute about lookin' like you just got out of the penitentiary."

"C'mon, Lawana. You're startin' to sound like my mama."

"Well, I'm not your mama! If you want to go get somethin' to eat with me you're gonna pull your pants up and change your appearance."

QJ reluctantly complied. The two of them left the house and drove a few miles away to a local soul food restaurant.

If Lawana and QJ had stuck around for ten more minutes they would have seen Terry coming. The shiny silver-colored Cadillac Escalade with the 22" chrome rimmed wheels cruised down the street slow and bold. The SUV was so wide that it nearly swiped the side mirrors on the parked cars that aligned the narrow street.

If Terry's car could talk it would have told the inexpensive Honda Accord it passed and the old rusty Cutlass Supreme sitting on bald tires belonging to Carmen's neighbor, to get the hell out of the way.

The car couldn't actually speak—it didn't have to. The owner's attitude did all the talking. The look on Terry's face screamed of pretentiousness. Onlookers weren't acknow-ledged. Head nods were shot back at anyone who dared to wave or point. It was the arrogance that Terry wore like a badge of honor that prompted QJ to tell his mother to search for someone else to refer to as her soul mate.

Terry had invested enough time and energy into Carmen that eliminated the need to ring the doorbell. A year earlier, before QJ discovered that his father was still alive, Carmen went to a nearby Wal-Mart and had an extra house key created just for Terry—against QJ's wishes.

The day she made this monumental decision, QJ protested vehemently.

"Why are you getting an extra key made?" QJ asked his mother. "Did you lose yours?"

"No," Carmen replied, preferring not to explain herself to her child.

"I didn't lose my key. Are you making one for Lawana?"

"No," Carmen replied, keeping her eyes focused on the street.

"Well, why are you getting an extra key?"

"It's for Terry," Carmen finally admitted without looking at her snooping son.

"Terry! Why?"

"Because I want to."

"Because you want to? So, you're just giving out keys to our house to strangers without running it by me? I live there too."

Carmen immediately pulled over to the side of the street, and finally looked her son in the eyes.

"Let me say something to you, and I want you to listen good," Carmen stated, the veins in the side of her neck pulsated and protruded to the point that QJ knew what he was about to hear from his mother wouldn't be pleasant.

"Mama, that's my house too," said QJ. "My daddy left that house for both of us not just for you. Terry doesn't need a key."

"What?"

"You heard me," QJ boldly replied. "That's my house too. I should…"

Before the flippant teen could utter another word, Carmen struck QJ across his lips with the back of her right hand. The gum QJ was chewing flew out of his mouth and stuck on the head rest of his seat.

"That is *my* fucking house!" Carmen shouted. "As long as you have breath in your body don't you ever part your lips to tell me anything about what your daddy supposedly left for us!"

"I pay the mortgage on *my* house! I buy the food that goes inside of the refrigerator that's inside *my* house. I buy the detergent that goes inside the washing machine inside of *my* house—the same washing machine that's used to wash your dirty-ass drawers. So, until you pay for something inside of *my* house, you will shut the hell up, and keep your comments about the keys to my house to yourself. Do you understand me?"

QJ was too busy whisking his tongue around the inside of his mouth to make sure all of his teeth were still intact to answer his mother's question.

"Boy, do you hear me talkin' to you?"

QJ didn't answer. He just used his tongue to poke around his inner lip to assess the damage. Carmen's backhand created a one inch gash in his bottom lip. Based on the look on her face and the way she was positioning her hand again, any further delay in QJ's response would lead to a second strike.

"Yeah, I hear you," QJ mumbled.

"Your daddy left us that house," Carmen stated, repeating her son's comment. "Let me tell you something. We wouldn't be living in that house if it wasn't for Terry's help. Remember when I lost my job because I'd missed too many days? By the way, those absentees were the result of you screwing up in school. It was Terry who paid the mortgage on that house for two straight months.

"All you do at that house is eat, sleep, and shit. You don't even cut the grass unless I make you. I'll give a key to whomever I want to, and you will keep your damn opinions to yourself."

That was the first and last discussion the two of them had about Carmen's decision to give Terry a house key. QJ had no choice but to suck it up, and deal with the fact that Terry was no longer required to ring the doorbell before entering.

"Hey, boo," Carmen said as she saw Terry come through the door.

"Hey, baby girl."

The couple hugged and then Terry planted a soft kiss on Carmen's luscious lips. She sighed softly as Terry palmed and gently squeezed her soft butt.

"How was your day?"

"Long and hard. I got threatened by a customer and then chastised by my boss," Carmen replied.

"Long and hard? Are you describing your day or what you need?" Terry asked flirtatiously.

"Stop being silly," Carmen replied, and then playfully slapped Terry on the arm. "On top of all that, my Blackberry started acting crazy. The screen went blank. I need to get it fixed."

"I have a cell phone you can use. It was given to me by my employer. I don't use it because it's kind of old, and I prefer my own. It's been sitting in the glove compartment of my car for months."

"Is it active?"

"It works, but I don't use it. The company pays for the first 100 minutes I use, and then I have to pay for every minute used after that."

"Cool," Carmen replied. "I doubt if I will use up 100 minutes. I just need to use it until my phone gets fixed—it should only take a few days."

"Okay," Terry replied, and then left out to retrieve it.

Meanwhile, QJ and Lawana were walking into a family-owned restaurant a few miles away. It was quaint, small, and more intimate than the typical New Orleans hole in the wall.

"Hello, Lawana," said the owner—who doubled as the host. "I see you have a date."

"Yeah, this is my godson. Do you have a table off in the corner somewhere so that we can talk?"

"Sure, I have the perfect spot for you. Follow me."

Lawana and QJ followed the large man to a table tucked away in the far corner of the small restaurant. It was obvious Lawana was a regular at the place because the waiters all smiled and waved as she passed.

"Here you go, pretty lady," he said, flashing a huge smile.

"Thank you," Lawana replied, avoiding eye contact with the man.

The owner's blatant flirtation with Lawana didn't go unnoticed by QJ.

"Damn, Lawana. That dude is sweatin' you," QJ said with a chuckle.

"Boy please! He can't do nothing for me, but get me a decent table. Besides, he ain't my type."

"He ain't your type? So you don't like the brotha's that look like they just got off the slave boat?"

"What?"

"That nigga's skin is so black if he didn't smile we'd probably mistake him for a shadow."

Lawana laughed. "He is dark—huh?"

"That dude is so dark he looks like he could have come over here on the Amistad," said QJ and then burst into laughter. "He definitely wanna get you somethin', but it ain't a table or anything on the menu here."

Lawana reached across the table and smacked QJ upside the head. "Boy stop being mannish! You think you can just say whatever you want to me? Don't make me pull off my shoe and put it on you, in here."

"Go head Lawana. You know I'm just playin' with you. Besides, I ain't gonna mess with you no more. You might go get B.A.M. to beat me up."

"Who is B.A.M.?"

"Your boyfriend over there...Black As Midnight!"

The two of them cracked jokes at some of the patrons for a few more minutes before ordering. QJ really did view Lawana as a second mother. She was the one person on the planet, besides his mother, whom he'd fight to his death trying to defend.

Small talk reigned for the first thirty minutes of their outing as Lawana searched for the perfect opportunity to breach the sensitive topic of Quincy's reemergence.

While QJ annihilated the catfish on his plate, Lawana decided it was time to dive into the topic.

"QJ, can I talk to you about somethin'?"

"What's up?"

"Umm, it's kind of touchy, but I want to talk to you about your father."

QJ stopped chewing. He took a swig of his soda and then leaned back in his chair.

"What about him?"

"Well, your mom told me you saw him."

"I'll bet she did. Did she also tell you she's been lying to me all these years? She told me he was dead."

"Where did you see him?"

QJ looked at his drink. Lawana could tell by the young boy's facial expression that this conversation was going to be anything but smooth.

"QJ, I asked you a question. When and where did you see Quincy?"

"I saw him under the Claiborne Avenue Bridge. He got into a fight with Bookie."

"A fight!" Lawana exclaimed. "How in the hell did he get into a fight with Bookie? And why are you still hangin' with that little criminal? I thought I told you stay away from that hoodlum."

"There you go—dissin' my boys again. Do you want me to tell you what happened or you wanna talk about Bookie?"

"Go ahead and tell me what happened," Lawana answered, rolling her eyes as she took a sip of her drink. "I still don't like that little bastard."

"He got into a fight with Bookie after Bookie messed with his shopping cart."

"His shopping cart?"

"Yeah, you know all those homeless people have shopping carts they put all that junk in. Anyway, Bookie was messin' with my dad's… I mean, ol' boy's cart. The next thing I knew they were scrappin'. Me and Tweety jumped in."

"Tweety was there too? I should have known. Those two boys are heading straight to the penitentiary and they're gonna take your ass right with them."

QJ didn't reply. He knew better than to get flippant with Lawana. The last time he disrespected her she smacked him so hard across the face that his speech was slurred for an entire day. He was talking like that Star Wars character, Jar Jar Binks.

"Finish," Lawana insisted. "How did you go from fighting to learning that he was your dad?"

QJ took a deep breath and continued his story.

"I was about to hit him with a pipe…"

"You were about to do what?" Lawana asked, and then leaned across the table with her fist clinched, ready to strike QJ in the chest.

QJ leaned backwards. "I didn't say that I hit him, I said I was about to hit him. I stopped when he called out my name."

Lawana sat back down in her chair. She took her napkin and wiped her lips.

"Finish."

"He called my name. I was shocked. I just stood there. The next thing I knew, he was tellin' me about my mama. He said he gave her the nickname Cookie."

Lawana shook her head in agreement. If she had any remaining thoughts that maybe this was all a case of mistaken identity, QJ's comments removed them.

"He told me he was my dad."

"What did you do?"

"The police were coming so I ran. He told me to run into the projects."

"Quincy told you to run into the projects?"

"Yeah, he told me where to go to get away from the cops."

Lawana may not have been a fan of Quincy's, but she recognized the significance of him helping QJ escape the police. That gesture was fueled by love—a father's love.

She took one last sip of her drink. She was about to suggest that they leave, but QJ had a different plan. If he had to answer Lawana's questions, he felt it was only right that she answer his.

"So, did you know he was alive all of these years?" QJ asked, and stared deep into his godmother's eyes.

Rarely did Lawana display nervousness when asked a question. In fact, you'd probably stand a better chance of catching a glimpse of Big Foot or the Loch Ness monster. But, QJ's question had her squirming like a worm on hot concrete.

"QJ, I have a confession. That lie she told you is partially my fault."

"What do you mean?"

"I encouraged your mom to tell you Quincy was dead."

Harmony gave way to tension as QJ became visibly disturbed by Lawana's admission.

"Damn, Lawana. I can't believe you played me like that."

"Look QJ, we lied to you to protect you from the truth. Your daddy left you and your mama. He started doing drugs and drinking and his entire personality changed.

"Was it the right thing to do? I don't know. But, it seemed like the best way to avoid telling you the truth."

"I don't believe he just left us for no reason. Why did he leave?"

"It's a long story QJ. Your dad became angry with your mom about something that happened."

"What did she do?"

Lawana was starting to regret her decision to get involved in this touchy issue. She checked her watch and decided it was time to go.

"It's not my place to say what happened."

"Why not? You wanted to talk—let's talk," QJ replied.

"You and your mom need to sit down and go over everything that transpired. All I want to say to you is that your mother loves you. Over the years I've watched her put her needs on the backburner so that you can have all the things you needed and most of the stuff you wanted.

"Your mom worked two and sometimes three jobs just to take care of you. She didn't have any support from your dad. I know you are angry with her, but it's important that you don't lose sight of that."

QJ heard every word, but avoided eye contact with Lawana.

"When you needed someone to get you out of that Juvenile Detention Center last year, your mama was there harassing that judge to give you a break. She spent her life savings on lawyer fees.

"When those hoodlums were threatening you, your mom was the person marching across town into the St. Bernard projects to speak to their parents. Don't forget all the stuff she's done to protect you—stuff that your daddy should have been around to do."

Lawana's points were valid; so valid that QJ didn't have a rebuttal. His appetite vanished. His emotions were once again swirling inside. He partially understood his mother's decision, but he still wanted to know the whole story behind his parent's break up.

The two of them left the restaurant and went back to QJ's house. The ride home was quiet. Lawana felt like she'd at least made a cogent argument for QJ to be civil to his mother. All she could do at that point was hope that her comments would cause the impressionable teenager to rethink his position.

As they turned onto QJ's street, the setting evening sun made the 22" rims on Terry's Cadillac Escalade gleam like the high beam headlights on a car. The SUV was parked in the driveway. The expression on QJ's face was so disturbing, Lawana thought the boy was going to jump out of her moving car and run the other way.

Lawana rolled her eyes. Terry's presence at that moment could only nullify any headway she may have made with QJ that evening.

"I see Terry's here," said Lawana, in an attempt to gauge the boy's disposition.

"Terry's always here—that's the problem," QJ replied.

"QJ, I know you don't like it, but you are going to have to accept the fact that your mom is in love."

"They're both fake. She changes when Terry is around. Now all she wants to do is go to church. She was never into church before."

"QJ, there is nothing wrong with your mama wanting to go to church. You should be happy that she has someone in her life that encourages her to attend church. Truth be told, you should have your butt there every Sunday with them.

"I want you to go into that house and talk to your mom like you have some sense. Leave that nasty attitude on the porch. You need to show more respect."

QJ didn't reply. He looked out of the window as he contemplated whether or not to go inside.

"QJ, I'm talking to you. Do you understand what I'm saying?"

"Umm hmm."

"Umm hmm? Boy I will knock you out! You'd better answer me like you have some sense."

"Yes."

"That's better. Now give me a hug, and go inside and talk to your mom."

QJ gave Lawana a hug and exited the vehicle. He paused for a moment when he got to the front steps and turned around. Lawana was still parked outside. She rolled down her passenger window and shouted, "Boy, take your little narrow ass inside!"

QJ begrudgingly walked up the stairs and into the house. He'd heard every word his godmother said, and was going to try to control his emotions.

As he approached the top of the stairs he called out, "Mama!"

QJ heard his mother answer, "Yes, baby!"

He walked slowly up the stairs. He so desperately wanted to have a conversation about his dad, but deep down he was afraid. Afraid he might hear some things that weren't too flattering. Afraid he'd walk away from the discussion in an even fouler mood than when it started.

Nevertheless, he had to know more. It's only natural that this 15 year old child would want to know all he could about his father. He'd seen episodes of The Cosby Show, and often wished he could have a relationship with a man that resembled the one portrayed by Cliff and Theo.

This was the moment of clarity. All of his questions were about to be answered. He was going to ignore Terry long enough to whisk his mother away so that they could have a heart-to-heart discussion.

"Mama," QJ called out again as he approached his mother's room.

"Yes!" Carmen shouted once more.

Carmen's bedroom door was partially open so QJ entered without knocking. Not a wise decision. The back of Carmen's naked body was facing the bedroom door. She was holding onto the headboard of her bed while she straddled Terry's face. Her hips rotated like a belly dancer's hips. Beads of perspiration dominated her shoulders and back. Her head was positioned upwards, but she wasn't looking at the ceiling. Her eyes were closed tight as she welcomed Terry's snake like tongue.

Carmen never heard QJ. She was shouting *yes*, but it wasn't in acknowledgement of her son's presence. She was shouting *yes* because she was enjoying the multiple orgasms that were surging through her loins.

QJ stood there for a few seconds. He was in shock. He was enraged. He was embarrassed. He was hurt. He needed to talk, but his stressed out mother needed to cum.

QJ ran down the stairs and out the front door. Carmen was in so much ecstasy that she didn't see him standing in the doorway. She was too focused on *getting hers* to notice her son's presence, but she did hear the front door slam. Unbeknownst to her, the slamming of that door would serve as a metaphor for a dreadful turn in her and the confused child's relationship.

Chapter 6

A few days had passed since Lawana took QJ to dinner. She had been so busy at work that she hadn't called Carmen to find out how things turned out after she brought QJ home that evening.

Catching up with Carmen would have to take a back seat to Lawana's need to socialize over a few drinks. She stood in her master bedroom closet trying to decide what outfit to wear for her night out with the girls. After an hour of deliberation she chose a tan, linen pants suit with wide bottom legs. A brand new pair of black open-toe stilettos completed the outfit.

I sure hope this club Angela has been yapping about is worth it. If you've seen one Happy Hour, you've seen them all. Besides, I'm going to miss American Idol fooling around with her. Simon Cowell cracks me up — he handles those clowns the same way I would if I was a judge on that show.

Lawana grabbed her purse and dashed out the front door. It was already 7:00 P.M., the time she told Angela she'd meet her at Club Chameleon, but she was more than twenty minutes away.

The crowd entering and leaving the club seemed worthy of her time. The women were dressed sexy — like mature adults. Of course there were a few in their late 30's dressed like they were about to appear in a rap video, but they were few and far between.

The men were definitely appealing. No thirty year old men struggling to escape their youth wearing tennis shoes and baseball caps. The parking lot was filled well groomed men wearing squared toed hard heel shoes, nice fitting jeans, and blazers — real grown and sexy.

Lawana paid the $10 to enter and with her cell phone pressed against her ear tried to filter out the loud music so that she could hear Angela give her directions to her booth. After getting turned around a few times, Lawana finally saw Angela sitting in a far corner of the club at a booth.

"Girl, this place is packed," Lawana sat down.

"I told you this was the spot," Angela replied, bobbing her head to the Jill Scott tune bumping in the speakers.

"I see you wasted no time getting your drink on. You've already ordered your second drink."

"That one is for you," Angela replied. "I got you an Apple Martini. I know that's your drink."

"Thanks," Lawana replied, and then took a sip. "So, how many times have you come here?"

"This is my second time. I came here two weeks ago with Lisa. Giiirl, we didn't pay for one drink all night," said Angela, swaying side to side to the rhythm of the music. "You're lookin' cute. Watch... you won't have to spend a dime tonight. These brothas in here got money."

"I don't care how much money they have, you know I don't accept drinks from anyone. I order my own drinks. There are too many freaks out here slippin' shit in drinks these days."

Angela nodded in agreement, but she didn't reply. After hearing Lawana's comment she didn't dare tell Lawana that the drink she was sipping on had been purchased by a man standing near the bar eyeballing them.

"I wonder why they named this placed Club Chameleon. That's an odd name to for a club," Lawana commented as she looked around.

"Isn't it obvious," Angela replied. "Take a closer look. Things aren't always what they appear."

Lawana looked around and saw several men and women socializing and dancing. Nothing unusual about that. But, the longer she looked the more she noticed something odd. At a few of the secluded circular booths she noticed men sitting together.

"They look a little too cozy over there."

"Now you're catchin' on," Angela said with a chuckle. "In here, everything goes. That's why they call it Club Chameleon—people let their hair down and change into who they really are when they come in here."

"Girl, you have me in a gay club?"

"It's not a *gay* club Lawana. A *gay* club is exclusive. This club is for heterosexuals, bi-sexuals, *and* gays. It's for everyone."

"Well it ain't for me. Even if I was interested in someone in here I'd be scared to talk to him."

"Girl, you are so damn closed minded," Angela replied. "Look, try not to run out while I go to the ladies room."

"I'm coming."

"No you're not. You gotta stay here so we don't lose our seats."

"Okay."

Angela left Lawana alone, and went to relieve herself of the martini she'd guzzled down. Lawana wanted to run after her, but she sat there like she was told. People watching was what Lawana did best so she got a kick out of scoping out the scene.

This place is a damn meat market. These brothas are like thirsty blood hounds in here. They don't give the women a chance to breathe. Some of them look desperate and some of them look downright weird.

Ummm, he's cute. And he's leaning on the wall alone. Now I would definitely give him some play. Tight fade hair cut. Nice blazer. Jeans fitting just right—not too tight and not too baggy. Crisp white shirt. Nice squared toed shoes... look like they could be a pair of Kenneth Coles or Cole-Hahn's. Yeah, that's what I'm talkin' 'bout.

Come on handsome look this way so I can give you that, come hither look. Shiiit, this may end up being my lucky night after all.

What… what the fuck! Oh my goodness. No he didn't. Lord please tell me I'm not witnessing this. Is he doing what I think he's doing? No he didn't. That nasty bastard is digging in his nose. If he digs any deeper he's going to lose his damn finger. Doesn't he realize he's in a public place?

Whew, I'm glad he didn't look this way. Oooh shit, I spoke too quickly. No, no, please don't. He's lookin' at me. No, no, please don't. Loooord, please don't let this nasty ma'fucka come over here. Awwh shit… he's coming. Angela where are you?

Time was running out for Lawana. Either she was going to sit there and deal with Booger Boy or she was going to get the heck out of there and worry about explaining it to Angela later.

Fortunately, she was saved by Angela's emergence.

"Hey, girl! What did I miss?" Angela said as she sat back down.

Before Lawana could reply, the nose picker was standing next to their table. Lawana quickly put her glass up to her lips so that she wouldn't have to acknowledge him.

"Hello, ladies?"

"Hi," Angela replied, with a big cheesy grin.

"My name is, Spencer," replied the tall handsome man. He extended his hand to shake Angela's. Lawana damn near spit out her drink all over the table. The man shook Angela's hand with the same hand he'd used to pick his nose.

"I'm Angela, and this is my girlfriend, Lawana."

Spencer extended his hand to shake Lawana's. Lawana stared at Spencer's hand—visions of his long index finger exploring his nose cavity caused her stomach to churn. She looked up at Spence and then at Angela as she struggled to fend off the laughter that was bubbling inside of her.

"Uhhh, no disrespect, but you are interrupting me and my lady," Lawana blurted out and grabbed Angela's hand.

Angela looked like she wanted to slap Lawana up side her head.

"Oh, my bad," Spencer replied. "I didn't realize you ladies were a couple."

"Yes, we are," Lawana snapped.

"My bad," Spencer replied, and held up his hands and leaned back signaling he was backing off.

As the nose picker walked away, Lawana burst into laughter.

"Bitch, have you lost your mind?" Angela shouted.

Lawana was laughing too hard to reply. She was leaning over in the booth. Onlookers probably thought she was trying to find something under the table.

"Lawana, why would you do that? That was one of the cutest guys in here."

Lawana started gesturing like she was digging inside her nose.

"What?" Angela asked.

Lawana's laughter attack returned. She extended her finger and started ramming it up and down towards her nose. Angela felt like she was playing charades.

"Girl, what are you trying to say? Is something wrong with your finger?"

Lawana regained her composure long enough to say, "Not mine – his."

"What? His finger was crooked?"

"No. He was digging," Lawana managed to get out.

"Digging for what?" Angela asked. Suddenly the light bulb in her head came on. "Hold up, I know you ain't tryin' to say that ma'fucka was picking his nose."

At this point, Lawana was literally lying on the seat laughing like she'd just watched Richard Pryor in concert. "He, he, he wasn't picking, he was digging in his nose like he had gold in it," Lawana blurted out, her laughter barely made her words discernable.

"Ugggh!" Angela screamed. "Bitch you let me shake his hand and you knew he probably had boogers still dangling on it!'

Angela grabbed her Apple Martini and poured it on her hand. She then took the napkins that accompanied both of their drinks and started scrubbing her hand. She looked like a surgeon washing up before entering the operating room.

"Lawana, this shit ain't funny!" Angela yelled, as she herself let out a chuckle. "Bitch, I'm gonna get you back if it's the last thing I do. I'm gonna find a nigga that's digging in his ass and send him your way."

Angela's hand was now sticky from the alcohol. She threw the napkins at Lawana and stood up. "I gotta go to the ladies room and clean up. Bitch I'm telling you now, you'd better watch your back."

Lawana spent the next few seconds wiping the tears from her eyes. She knew she should have warned Angela, but it all happened so fast. Before she could say anything, Angela was already exchanging pleasantries with the guy.

Lawana flagged down a waitress and ordered more drinks for she and Angela. That was the best laugh she'd had in years. The more she thought about it, she realized she'D gotten even with Angela for the stunt she and Lisa pulled at the strip club a few weeks earlier.

As she waited for their drinks to arrive, Lawana resumed her people watching session.

Let's see what I can spot now. Damn, since when do men dance together in groups? That's some real gay shit. And then they can't dance. Bless her heart over there. Her man is standing there with his arm wrapped around her waist while slipping his phone number to her girlfriend... and that scandalous heifer is grinning and accepting the number. I should go over and bust both of their asses out. No Lawana, mind your business. Sooner or later homegirl will find out on her own.

Look at those two over there. They need to get a damn room. I know it's dark in here, but it ain't that damn dark. She might as well stretch across the table and spread her legs in front of everyone the way she's allowing herself to be fondled.

Suddenly, the combination of laughter and alcohol that had lightened Lawana's mood was stifled. Frown lines became so pronounced on her forehead that they looked like they'd been drawn on with a Sharpie. Lawana squinted harder at the couple canoodling in the corner. She wasn't sure if her eyes were playing tricks on her.

Hold up. Hold the fuck up! I know that ain't who I think it is. Oh hell no! That low down, sneaky…

"I'm tellin' you right now, Lawana this ain't over!" said Angela as she sat back down.

Lawana was so busy spying that she didn't even acknowledge her friend.

"Oh, hell no! This shit ain't goin' down like this," Lawana mumbled.

Angela saw the look on Lawana's face and instantly knew something was wrong. "What's up? What are you talkin' 'bout?"

"I'll be right back," Lawana replied and then walked towards the ladies room. She stood in the area right outside the entrance to the ladies room and pulled out her cell phone.

"C'mon Cee… answer the phone," she mumbled as she paced back and forth.

"Hello."

"Hey, girl. What's up?"

"Nothin' much. I'm just sittin' here eating popcorn and watching the soap operas I recorded earlier while I was at work. What's all that noise?"

"Oh, that's just the music. I'm in this new club Angela brought me to."

"Well, it must be garbage if you're callin' me from the club."

"Yeah, it's kind of wack. This guy was bothering me so I just called you so that he could get the hint that I didn't want to be bothered."

"Don't be using me to scare away men."

"Girl, I had to do it. So where is my godson?"

"Upstairs playin' that video game—like always."

"I'm surprised you ain't kickin it with Terry tonight."

"Nope. I'm chillin' alone tonight. I don't want any company; I just wanna watch my stories."

"I feel you, girlfriend. Well don't let me stop you. Go do your thing."

"Alright. You be careful out there. There are some crazy ass men hangin' in those clubs."

"I hear you. You know I keep my pistol loaded and under my car seat. I'll talk to you later."

"Okay. I love you."

"I love you too. Kiss QJ for me."

"Okay."

Lawana hung up and threw her cell phone inside her purse. She paced back and forth a little longer as she tried to figure out her next move.

"Hey, sexy," said a guy standing a few feet away. "Can I buy..."

"You can't buy a damn thing for me!" Lawana barked. "Actually, you can leave me the hell alone, right now."

The guy took a few steps backwards. "Damn, bitch. I was just tryin' to holla at you."

"Your snaga-tooth mama's a bitch!" Lawana replied; mean mugging the flirt like he'd just pinched her butt.

The guy walked away, and it was good he did; Lawana wasn't in the mood for socializing. She wanted to fight. She went into the ladies room and entered an open stall so that she could think better.

I'm going to break that shit up. If I have to pull off my earrings and fight, then so be it.

Lawana stormed out of the stall and marched back into the club. She was eager to get to Terry, but the encounter came quicker than she expected. As soon as she re-entered the club area she walked right into her foe.

"Whoa… look who we have here. If it isn't Ms. Lawana. Ms. Sexy Ass Lawana."

"You're damn right, and I saw you hiding in that corner booth with that skank!"

"Awwh, that ain't nothin'. She's just a friend."

"Just a friend? Have you forgotten that you're dating my best friend?"

"No, I haven't forgotten. We were just sitting there having drinks."

"Bullshit! You had your tongue shoved down her throat!"

"Calm down," Terry replied, in a condescending tone. "If I didn't know any better I'd think you were jealous."

"Jealous?"

"Yeah, jealous," said Terry with a chuckle. "I've seen you peeking at me from time to time. You want some of this tongue too—don't you?"

"I wouldn't let you lick the bottom of my shoe with your tongue."

"So, now what? You gonna go run and tell Carmen?"

"I ain't gonna run and tell Carmen anything… you are."

"Excuse me?"

"You heard me. Today is Wednesday, you have until Saturday to tell Carmen or else I will."

"Girl, you're crazy."

"You ain't seen crazy. If you don't come clean you're gonna see crazy."

"And who do you think Carmen is going to believe?"

"Carmen has been my best friend long before your sorry ass came around."

"That may be true, but I got that ass on lock. She ain't gonna believe your story over mine."

Lawana inched closer to Terry. "You have three days. If you think I'm playin'—try me."

Lawana turned and walked away, not bothering to say "excuse me" to the waitress she nearly knocked down. Terry stood there for a few seconds — surprised and pissed off.

Chapter 7

There are some things in life that are inexplicable. They defy logic. Like a humans natural tendency to love someone that doesn't love them back. Or the perplexing reality that sometimes, many underhanded and disingenuous people seem to receive blessings, while honest and prayerful people sometimes struggle no matter how much they ask God for help.

A child's willingness to forgive, and look past the faults of the most neglectful parent, ranks right up there with some of life's most baffling occurrences.

Since reconnecting with Quincy, QJ couldn't stop thinking about the man he was named after. Visions of his father's face dominated his dreams. The sound of his voice awakened him from deep slumbers. Thoughts of the relationship they could have had, and could potentially still have, were firmly entrenched in the forefront of his mind.

The desire to know what caused his parents to break up also consumed him. The thought of his mother being forever connected to Terry scared him. Images of his mother and father sharing intimate moments while he stood in the background smiling and basking in the moment became commonplace. If those images were ever going to become a reality, QJ knew he needed to have his toughest questions answered.

Friday morning came swiftly. Although the sun didn't make its presence known until 6:00 A.M., QJ had already been pacing around his room a full hour earlier.

I gotta go confront him. I'm gonna head to Palmer Park this evening after school. The park ain't that big so he shouldn't be hard to find. I may go all the way over there, and he might not be there. Oh well, if he ain't there I'll wait around until he shows up.

As soon as school let out that afternoon, QJ headed to the bus stop. Today was arguably the most important day of his life. The day he was going to find out the truth. Lawana was hesitant to tell him. His mother was clearly uncomfortable talking about the past. Quincy was his last hope.

Quincy and Scoop were in the park playing chess on a makeshift board. A long sheet of paper from a discarded sketch pad served as their chess board. Quincy took a marker and drew black and white squares on the paper. Discarded bottle tops served as the chess pieces. Scoop used a marker to write letters on the top of each bottle top to identify the pieces. The letter R was scribbled on the top of a few pieces to symbolize a Rook. The letters PA were used to symbolize the Pawns and so forth.

Chess is the ultimate thinking man's game. The strategy required to play provided the perfect mental stimulation for a thinker like Quincy. Despite his lack of cerebral acuity, Scoop was surprisingly good at the game.

Quincy was two moves away from capturing Scoop's King. Scoop had lost three games in a row so he was taking his time before he moved. His basketball career may have ended years earlier, but the competitor in him was still alive and kicking.

"Damn, bruh. It's been five minutes. When are you gonna move?" Quincy asked.

"Man, be quiet," Scoop barked. "I'm tryin' to concentrate. That's how you've been beatin' me. You're always tryin' to distract a nigga."

"Yeah, right," Quincy replied, and shook his head.

Quincy looked around the park while he sat there contemplating his next move. Quincy noticed a short stocky man walking his way.

"Who is that?" he asked.

Scoop looked up and then put his head back down. "That's the dude I was tellin' you about the other day. The dude that's always comin' around offerin' to help cats like you and me get clean."

Quincy looked the man up and down as he approached. He looked more like a used car salesman than some type of counselor.

"Hello," the man said as he walked up smiling from ear to ear. "Who's winning?"

Scoop didn't look up. He just pointed at Quincy.

"Hi. My name is Terrance Lock. I am a member of Ebenezer Baptist Church. The church is located a few miles up the street. I'm sure Scoop has told you about me."

Quincy didn't respond. He just puffed on his cigarette and nodded.

"I want to offer you an opportunity to attend one of our H.A.B.U. meetings," Terrance said, and handed Quincy a business card. "H.A.B.U. stands for Help A Brotha Up. It's an extension of our Men's Group at the church. We focus on helping brotha's who may have fallen on hard times, get their lives together. We offer counseling, drug rehabilitation, and even a place to stay if you remain in the program long enough."

Quincy wasn't that interested until he heard the part about getting a place to stay. Palmer Park was okay for the time being, but it didn't beat staying somewhere with a roof.

Quincy looked at the card, and nodded. He never uttered a word. In fact, he didn't really make much eye contact. He just stared at the card, and thought about QJ.

I miss my son. This could be my first step to getting my son back... maybe even getting Carmen back.

Terrance had approached enough homeless men to know when he had a man's attention. Those who weren't interested would walk away and sometimes refuse to take his business card—that's how Scoop acted towards him. But, Quincy was different. His body language suggested that he wanted to clean up, but like so many junkies, he didn't know how.

"What's your name?"

"Quincy."

"Well Quincy, there is no pressure my man. Just think about it. I'll be back next week. Maybe we can talk or somethin'."

Quincy nodded again. "We'll see."

Terrance turned and walked away. Quincy stared at the card again. Scoop was still focused on making his next move, but that didn't stop him from commenting.

Without looking up from the chess board he said, "I don't have a reason to clean up. You do."

Scoop left the park after conceding victory to Quincy. He didn't handle losing well so he decided to take a walk. Quincy opted to tend to his hygiene as the evening sunset cast shadows around the park.

He opened up a small brown bag containing a rag and a tooth brush Scoop had given him his first day at the park. He used water from a bottle he'd been sipping on to wet the corner of the towel. He then took the soap and lathered the towel.

He loosened the top buttons on his shirt and then stuck his hand inside of his shirt and washed his arm pits. After a few seconds of scrubbing he then unzipped his pants and stuck the damp towel in between his legs to wash his crotch.

Once finished, he used the remaining contents of the water bottle to rinse the soap out of the towel. Back inside the brown bag went the soap and towel.

Quincy returned to his corner of the park and sat down on the ground next to the tree. He paused for a moment to check above his head and the surrounding area for the huge caterpillars that often hung down from the leaves. He had no idea what type of caterpillars they were, but he knew they had a mean bite.

He pulled out a newspaper and held it up to his face. Quincy liked to read the newspaper from front to back. It had less to do with his thirst for knowledge and more to do with the fact that the entire process took nearly two hours — a great way to kill time.

"What's up?" someone asked.

Quincy lowered his newspaper to see who had ventured into his domain. His eyes became as large as stop signs when he saw that it was his son, QJ. Nervousness took over. His hands started to shake as evident by the crinkling sound of the newspaper.

"Hey QJ," Quincy replied hesitantly. "Lets sit over there and talk."

They moved over to the bench and sat down. Quincy nibbled on his bottom lip while he searched for the right words. The appropriate words were hard to retrieve so he settled for a safer subject.

"How is your mama?"

"What?"

"Your mama, how is she doing?"

"She's cool."

"You look a lot like her. Is she remarried?"

"What?"

"Damn boy, you can't hear? I asked if your mama remarried."

"No."

"Is she dating?"

"Yeah. She's talking about getting married or something."

"Do you get along with her fiancé?"

"No."

"Why?"

QJ grew tired of his father's snooping so he cut Quincy's inquisition short. "Look man, I didn't come here to tell you all of my mama's business."

"So, why did you come?" Quincy replied defensively.

"I just wanna know one thing. Why did you leave?"

"What?" Quincy mumbled.

"Why did you leave us?" QJ asked again, his tone dripping with anger. "How could you just up and leave your family? A real man wouldn't do that."

Quincy put his head down. Staring at the ants scurrying in the dirt was more pleasant at that moment than looking into his child's pain stricken eyes.

"QJ, it's not that simple."

"What do you mean it's not that simple?"

"It's not that simple, son."

"Bullshit!" QJ yelled, his emotions getting the best of him.

Quincy was taken aback by his son's remark, but he knew he had no choice but to deal with QJ's outburst. Disrespect is another byproduct of absenteeism.

"QJ, I know it's hard for you to understand, but believe me when I tell you, there is more to the story than meets the eye."

"Yeah right," QJ replied in a sarcastic tone, accompanied by a dismissive hand gesture.

Quincy looked over at QJ and saw him use his shirt sleeve to wipe a tear from his cheek. He'd fought back the urge to defend his actions since he and QJ reconnected. Unfortunately, his reluctance to tell his side of the story was putting him in a deeper credibility hole with QJ.

It was time to set the record straight. Time for him to stop trying to protect Carmen. The time had come to face his past.

Quincy's leg twitched excessively. His nerves were in a frenzy. He was so nervous that he started licking his parched lips. They were still as dry as sandpaper.

An awkward silence set in. The cars speeding down Carrollton Avenue seemed to slow down and coast like they were cruising through a school zone. The crickets that were chirping loud enough to give an aspirin a headache put a hold on communicating for the moment. Even Mother Nature got involved—commanding the wind to cease and desist its whistling so that she could hear Quincy's testimony.

"When we were together your mother and Lawana were best friends and hanging out all the time. I was cool with their friendship. At the time I was starting a new job at City Hall and it was taking up a lot of my time. I was so busy that I had to take a lot of work home. So, even my days off were like regular work days for me.

"There were a lot of things your mom would need to get done, you know, errands and stuff. She was too busy watching you to get those things during the day. Lawana did a lot of those things that your mom couldn't do. I was cool with that because it took a lot of pressure off of me.

"Anyway, when you were around three years old, I noticed that your mama and Lawana started hangin' out a lot more. Things had sort of calmed down for me at work, so I was able to be home with you more. I felt your mom needed some time to relax and socialize since she'd spent so much time lookin' after you.

"Well, at first your mama, Lawana, and some of their other girlfriends would go to Happy Hours and stuff like that to have a few drinks. I was cool with that until one night your mom came home at about 3:00 A.M.

"She tried to sneak and get into bed, but I was awake. That pissed me off. That made me suspicious because I don't feel there is any reason for a married woman to be hangin' out past midnight. I figured she must have been out doing somethin' she had no business doing. Combine that with the fact that I never really trusted Lawana, and I felt like somethin' was going on.

"That's really when the distrust started between us. We were able to get past that little incident, but it definitely caused problems for us.

"When you were five years old, your mama and Lawana decided they wanted to go on a five day cruise to the Bahamas. I had a problem with that because I don't believe a married woman should be goin' on a cruise without her husband."

"Why didn't you go with her?" QJ asked.

"I wanted to, but your mama didn't want me to. She insisted that only her girlfriends were going. They weren't bringing their men, so there was no need for me to come. That sent up another red flag."

"What does that have to do with you abandoning us?" QJ asked, clearly getting agitated by how long it was taking Quincy to explain his position.

"I'm getting to that," Quincy replied, and then lit a cigarette. He took two long puffs before he continued.

"That cruise was the straw that broke the camel's back. When your mama returned from the cruise she was acting funny with me."

"How?" asked QJ, and then pulled out his own pack of cigarettes. He lit a cigarette and started puffing it like Quincy wasn't sitting there next to him.

Quincy was surprised by his son's total disregard for him. He felt that QJ's willingness to smoke in front of him was disrespectful, but he didn't feel empowered to chastise the 15 year old.

"Ummm," Quincy mumbled, struggling to refocus. "Your mama wouldn't let me touch her. She wouldn't kiss me and refused to be intimate. She wasn't that way before she left for the cruise so I found it odd that she would be that way after she returned.

"My instincts told me that something happened on that cruise. About three or four days after your mama and I made love, my suspicions were proven."

"What happened? Did some man call the house? Did her girlfriend's snitch? What happened?" QJ was eager to know, he started throwing questions at Quincy faster than he could answer them.

Quincy looked at QJ and then took a few more puffs of his cigarette. "Son, are you sure you want me to continue?"

QJ's heart was racing. His hand shook nervously as he put the cigarette to his lips and puffed. "Yeah, I wanna know."

"Well, about three days after we were intimate, I went to the bathroom and…"

"And what?"

"…your mama gave me Chlamydia."

"Chlamydia. What's that?"

"Son, your mama gave me the *clap*."

At that moment, a strong gust of wind swooped through the park. It was like Mother Nature's way of saying, "I'll be damn!" QJ was speechless. He smoked his cigarette all the way down to the filter—never once looking in Quincy's direction.

Quincy hated telling his son that, but it was the only way he could paint a picture of how bad things had gotten between him and Carmen.

"Son, are you okay?"

QJ continued to look in the other direction. It wasn't until he nodded that Quincy continued.

"I'm sure you can imagine how crazy things got after that. I confronted your mama, and at first she denied it. She tried to make it look like I'd been sleepin' around, but I knew for a fact that I wasn't. It took about a week, but she finally admitted that she'd hooked up with some dude she'd met on that trip. I guess she figured that what happened on that cruise ship would remain on that cruise ship."

"Is that why you left?"

"I just couldn't take it QJ. I was fucked up. Man, you don't understand how devastated I was. I loved your mama with all of my heart. You were conceived out of love, bruh. Taking care of you and your mama was all I thought about back then.

"I was depressed. I started drinkin' harder and then one night, I smoked crack with this cat I knew. I just needed to take away the pain. I just couldn't shake off the hurt. The drugs gave me some relief. Every time I looked at her I thought about what happened. She never really looked sorry. She never really apologized to me.

"Lawana didn't make things any easier. I confronted her, and she told me it wouldn't have happened if I had been handlin' my business. Man, I wanted to kill her and your mama."

Quincy looked over at QJ and was surprised to see him nodding his head in agreement. It was the first time QJ had even shown the slightest bit of understanding toward Quincy's position.

"The fact that she gave me the *clap* and didn't show any contrition..."

QJ looked confused for a moment. Quincy forgot he was talking to a kid. He also realized that his son probably wasn't the most studious kid around. He decided to dumb down his vocabulary.

"Your mama didn't act like she was sorry for what she'd done."

QJ's confused look was replaced with another head nod. Quincy managed to let out a little smirk once he saw the light bulb come on in his child's head. QJ had caught up with what he was saying.

"I couldn't live with her anymore. I felt totally disrespected. I didn't know what to do. That depression was kicking my ass. Before I knew it I was drinking more and then smoking more and more crack to try to numb the pain.

"Things just kept getting worse. One day your mama came home from work early and saw me cookin' crack in the kitchen."

"You were cookin' crack in our house?" asked QJ.

"Yeah, it got that bad," Quincy admitted reluctantly. "She told me to leave and don't come back until I got cleaned up. We argued for a little bit, and then that kind of blew over. I didn't even leave that night. But a few days later, I just got up in the middle of the night and left. When I left I never came back."

"So, you're sayin' she made you leave?"

"Well, I guess it depends on how you look at it. She kept tellin' me to leave and don't come back until I got cleaned up. Considering what she did to me, I didn't feel she was in any position to be tellin' me to leave the house that I bought.

"I'm not sayin' I'm right, but at the time it all went down I felt like she should have left the house. She was the one who cheated. She was the one who brought home a venereal disease. She was the one who refused to apologize for what she'd done. Yeah I was wrong for cookin' that shit in the house, but she was wrong too.

"Even though I was crushed, I never tried to put your mama out. Don't get it twisted, a part of me wanted her to leave, but I never tried to force her out. I loved her. All I wanted from her was an apology. All I wanted was some type of explanation. I didn't even get that from her."

"But what about me? When you left and didn't come back, did you even think about me?" QJ asked, not bothering to hide his tears. That rough and tough exterior he'd been walking around with started to peel away like cheap paint on an old house.

Quincy placed his hand on his son's shoulder as he struggled to fight back his own tears.

"Son, I never forgot about you. I watched you even when you didn't know you were being watched. I saw your first fight."

"What?"

"You heard me; I saw your first fight. You were on the school playground at recess. You were around seven years old. Y'all were playing kick ball, and you kicked the ball and it hit that little boy in the face. I saw the whole thing. I used to stand outside the school playground in the far corner and watch you at recess everyday."

"Gerald," QJ said and smirked. "His name was Gerald."

"I was proud of you that day."

"Why? I got beat up."

Quincy laughed. "Yeah, he did whip you pretty good, but you didn't stop tryin' to get at him."

"Well, he probably wouldn't have whipped me if I had a daddy around to teach me how to fight."

QJ's comment hit Quincy harder than a punch to the gut.

"Touché," was all Quincy could say.

"*Too* what?" QJ asked. A confused look dominated his face again.

"Touché... that's French. In Fencing, the French say this when acknowledging a point being made."

"What's Fencing?" asked the confused child.

"Fencing is that sport when the people have on all white suits with a mask, and they are fighting each other with those swords."

"Oh yeah, I know what you're talkin' 'bout. I never knew it was called Fencing."

"Yeah, that's what it's called," Quincy replied amusingly. "Anyway, I was saying you made a good point. I should have been around to teach you how to fight."

Quincy pulled out his pack of cigarettes again, and in an odd move, offered QJ one. Dysfunctional by most standards, but it seemed like an appropriate peace offering considering he had nothing else to offer him.

QJ looked at his father, and then at the cigarette. Eventually he accepted the offer and placed the cigarette between his parted lips.

"QJ, the point I'm tryin' to make is that I've watched you grow up from afar. I was standing outside when you graduated from Elementary School. I was full of pride when I saw you that day in your little suit."

"Did my mama know you were there?"

"I think she did. She looked right at me. She may have recognized me. I don't know."

Quincy puffed on his freshly lit cigarette.

"I may not have been there physically, but I've always been watchin' you. I saw you that day under the bridge."

"What?"

"QJ, as big as this city is, do you think it's a coincidence that I just happened to be camped out a few feet away from where you and your crew hang out damn near everyday? I chose that spot because I knew that's where you hung out in the evening.

"There are no coincidences in life. Everything happens for a reason. Our talking here today was planned by The Man upstairs."

QJ looked stunned at his father's admission. He may not have been the sharpest pencil in the box, but he was astute enough to know what the admission implied.

"So you're tellin' me that all of these years I've been walkin' around thinkin' you were dead, you were close enough to make contact with me?"

"I didn't know your mama told you I was dead. She shouldn't have said that."

"She felt like she was protecting me. But, that ain't got nothin' to do with the fact that you could have reached out to me all those years and you didn't. You were mad at my mama, and you dissed me too. I'm not sayin' you didn't have a right to be mad at her, but you didn't have to abandon me."

Before Quincy could answer, their conversation was interrupted by Scoop. He'd walked off his chess loss and was ready to relax in the cool shade for the remainder of the evening.

"Wuz up?" Scoop shouted. "We got company?"

Quincy looked at Scoop and then back at QJ. He wanted to address QJ's last comment, but he knew Scoop wouldn't allow that to happen without interrupting.

"Look, can you come back tomorrow so we can talk some more? I wanna make sure you fully understand where I'm coming from," he asked.

"Nawh, don't worry about it. I understand more than you think," QJ replied, and then stood up and walked away.

As QJ walked away, Scoop took over the vacated spot on the bench. He pulled out a wrinkled cigarette.

"I would offer you one, but this is my last."

"It's all good."

"Let me guess; that was your son."

"Umm hmm," Quincy mumbled.

"So, he came here to see you?" asked Scoop.

"Yeah."

"He wanted some answers to questions that have been nagging him for years?" asked Scoop.

"Yeah. I don't think he was happy with what he heard," said Quincy.

"Do you think that matters?"

"Of course, it matters," Quincy replied in an aggravated tone.

"Probably doesn't matter as much as you think," Scoop replied, his head surrounded by a cloud of cigarette smoke.

"What?"

"Well, it matters, but not as much as you think."

"What? Man, you're tryin' to tell me that if you saw your pops after all these years you wouldn't care about his explanation for leaving?"

"I would a little. I mean, if I saw him I would ask him a few questions. But, I ain't gonna go lookin' for his ass to ask him a few questions. Nawh, dog. It doesn't work like that. If that kid came all the way over here to speak to you it's because he wanted to see you first and foremost. Getting a few questions answered is lagniappe."

"Dude, you're trippin. That boy hates me."

Scoop shook his head and stared at Quincy. He plucked the cigarette a few feet away, and then placed his hand on Quincy's shoulder.

"Listen up, grasshopper because I'm only going to say this once. That little boy misses his daddy. People don't go chasing people they hate just to get answers. If anything, they try to get as far away as possible.

"That is a kid who is growin' up in this rough-ass city without a father. Take it from a former ballplayer; the roughest little niggas on the team are the ones who need the most coaching. They actually gravitate to strong men that will guide them. That boy needs a strong man in his life.

Someone who can guide him like a strong coach guides his team to victory.

"He will be back—mark my words. When he comes back you gotta be ready for a challenge. He isn't gonna just change the way he's been livin' all these years, and start listening to you. You're gonna have to put in some work. The question is; when he comes back here lookin' for you again, are you gonna be the coach he needs or are you gonna drop the ball again?"

Scoop stood up and walked over to a clump of nearby shrubs where he hid his sleeping bag. Quincy continued to sit on the bench as he processed everything Scoop said.

"Now, I'm going to bed," Scoop called out. "Counseling your ass has got me drained. A nigga gotta recharge his batteries."

"Don't let the bed bugs bite," Quincy said jokingly.

"Too late, they been bitin' me," Scoop replied as he used his hand to swat away the bugs and debris on his bag. "I'll worry about my bed bugs; you worry about that little boy."

Quincy looked over his shoulder at Scoop and then nodded his head. His nod wasn't a hollow gesture; he was really feeling everything Scoop said.

"I'm serious, dog. I don't believe that boy hates you, but I can tell you this, if you don't step up to the plate now that he has opened the door, he will start hating you. As men— especially black men—we don't get too many opportunities to fix the shit we break. Nope, most of us have to figure out a way to get around in the pile of shit we create. You, my brotha, are gettin' a second chance. Don't fuck this up, dog."

Chapter 8

It was Sunday morning. Carmen and Terry made their customary trek to the 10:00 A.M. church service. Carmen was really beginning to enjoy church—thanks to Terry's encouragement. Prior to meeting Terry, Carmen would have been considered agnostic. It wasn't that she didn't believe in God, she just didn't believe there was a greater power that she could trust and rely on. Like many agnostics, she felt Christianity was a crutch used by those who didn't have the courage to face and deal with their own problems.

It was probably that belief that caused her to be so cold and callous in the way she treated people. There was no external motivator for her to show contrition. For a long time she believed that when things went wrong they eventually worked out. If it didn't work out, it was because it wasn't meant to work out. Apologies were unnecessary. If someone wronged you, you have a choice whether to deal with them or not. Whether a person apologizes for the wrong doing is irrelevant.

That was Carmen's philosophy and she made no apologies for it. It wasn't until she met Terry and was convinced to attend church that she learned that we have to atone for our wrong doings. She was still struggling with her inability to let go of grudges, but she was getting better at it.

Terry's dedication to attending church intrigued Carmen. Terry was involved in various ministries within the church, and was an all around active member. Carmen joined the church and was warming up to the idea of joining a ministry, but was reluctant to do it. Her primary goal was learning the principles of Christianity — joining a ministry would have to wait.

Carmen was still struggling to get QJ into church. The boy had absolutely no interest. The one time he did attend he wore baggy pants and a baseball cap. Terry told QJ to change his clothes, and when he refused, an argument ensued. Carmen never tried to make QJ attend again — it was just too much of a hassle.

The service was cool. Pastor Stud preached on the topic of forgiveness. The sermon spoke to Carmen's heart. She spent the entire service thinking about her life with Quincy, and how she behaved back then. She thought about the day he left, and her unwillingness to forgive him for leaving her and QJ. It was the first sermon that moved Carmen to tears.

"Are you okay?" Carmen asked, as they drove to her house. She noticed that Terry seemed a little distant before, during, and after service.

"I'm fine," Terry replied in a low tone.

It had been three days since Terry's spat with Lawana in that night club. Lawana was a hot head, and Terry knew it. If she said she was going to tell Carmen what she witnessed, it wasn't a bluff — Lawana was going to do it.

Terry watched Carmen closely. As long as Carmen was communicating and laughing, the coast was clear. If for some reason her mood changed on this sunny Sunday afternoon that meant Lawana had made good on her threat.

"Baby, you know what we should do? We should just turn off our cell phones, get some popcorn, and spend the entire day watching movies," Terry suggested, a desperate attempt to eliminate the possibility of Lawana reaching Carmen.

"That's a great idea!" Carmen replied. "I don't feel like cooking a big meal. I'll make some hot dogs. There are a couple of movies I've wanted to watch."

"Cool. We'll watch them," Terry replied, and winked.

When they entered the house, QJ was walking up the stairs eating a big bowl of cereal. He looked back at his mother and Terry and rolled his eyes. A few seconds later his bedroom door slammed.

Carmen knew her son's behavior was disrespectful. She ought to slap some sense into QJ, but she knew that was futile at this point. She turned to Terry and tried to change the subject.

"Don't worry about him baby. Let's just get ready to watch our movies," she said and planted a soft kiss on Terry's lips.

Terry went into the living room and plopped down on the sofa. Carmen walked over to the refrigerator and removed the hot dogs from the freezer. She grabbed a pot from under the sink, and filled it with water.

As she dumped a few hot dogs into the pot of water, her cell phone started to ring. Terry turned around immediately.

"Baby, I thought you were going to turn off your phone? I've already turned mine off."

"I am, baby. This is Lawana; let me see what she wants. This shouldn't take long."

"Shit," Terry mumbled.

"What's up, girl?" Carmen asked in a jovial tone.

"Hey, Cee. Are you busy?"

"Well not really, but we're about to watch some movies. You lucky you caught me because I was about to turn off my phone."

"Who are you watching movies with?"

"Terry, silly. Who else am I gonna be watchin' movies with?"

"Umm, can you go somewhere private to talk for a minute?"

Carmen could tell from Lawana's tone that something was wrong. "Umm yeah, is everything okay?"

"Carmen, I need you to go somewhere private so we can talk."

"Okay," Carmen replied as she walked outside on her porch. "I'm outside now. What's up?"

"Did Terry tell you about Thursday night?"

"No. What happened?"

"I don't know how to say this."

"Say what, Lawana? You've never been shy about sayin' what's on your mind so don't start now."

"I saw Terry at the club."

"What club?"

"Club Chameleon."

"Okay. I know Terry goes to hang out with friends."

"I saw Terry Thursday night hugged up and kissing on some woman. I made it clear that I would tell you what I saw. I was hoping y'all had discussed it by now."

Carmen stood there silently. She didn't know what to say. She knew Lawana didn't like Terry, but she wasn't expecting a phone call like this.

"Hello. Cee, are you still there?"

"Yeah, I'm still here," Carmen replied, not bothering to hide her anger.

"I know this is bad news, but you're my best friend. I had to tell you. God knows I didn't wanna have to make this call."

"Yeah, right," Carmen replied.

"Excuse me?"

"Lawana, you've been lookin' for a reason to break up my relationship with Terry from the start."

"What?"

"You heard me! You're getting' a kick out of this."

"Carmen, I've never hid the fact that I don't like Terry, but I would never make up a story like this to break y'all up."

"Whatever! You've *been* jealous of my relationship from the start. You don't have anyone special in your life so you're tryin' to shit on mine."

"What the fuck are you talkin' 'bout?"

"Why are you just callin' me today? It's Sunday, you said you saw Terry on Thursday. If you were so concerned about me, why did you wait three days to tell me this?"

"I waited because I told Terry's lowdown ass I would wait three days before I approached you. Carmen you need to open your eyes!"

"My eyes *are* open. You need to mind your own business. Don't call me with this messy shit! Those damn night clubs are dark, how do you know it was Terry? Knowing you, you were probably drunk."

"Cee, I know what I saw. Yeah, I was drinkin' but I wasn't drunk. Girl, you need to check yourself."

"No bitch, you need to check yourself! Don't call me with this bullshit. I didn't see it for myself so I don't want to entertain your gossip!"

"Bitch! Who you callin' a bitch? I'm tryin' to look out for your stupid ass! You're the one gettin' played!"

"No, I'm not gettin' played! You need to spend more time gettin' your own shit together. Terry warned me about you."

"What in the hell does that mean?"

"Terry told me how you flirt when you come over here. I didn't want to believe it so I never said anything to you about it."

"*I* flirt? Terry flirted with me!"

"I guess you were lookin' out for me when you failed to tell me that too. You are so fake, Lawana."

"I'm fake! Bitch, I was…"

"You know what? I don't want to hear nothing you have to say. I'm about to hang up."

"Carmen, if you hang up this phone, you don't have to bother ever callin' me again."

"That's fine with me," Carmen replied, and then hung up.

Carmen stood on the porch for nearly five minutes as she tried to recover from her argument with Lawana. A huge lump formed inside of her throat as she struggled to ignore Lawana's comments.

Lawana had been opinionated, catty, and a loud mouth, but she'd always gone out of her way to support and protect Carmen. Nevertheless, love is blind. Terry made Carmen feel special. When in Terry's presence, she felt like she was the most important woman on the planet. Lawana's comments totally contradicted those feelings.

Unbeknownst to Carmen, Terry was standing on the other side of the door listening to her discussion with Carmen. Like a true playa, an alibi was being crafted while Carmen and Lawana were arguing.

"Hey, baby. Are you okay?"

Carmen sat down on the wooden rocking chair on her porch. She used her shirt to wipe her face and tried her hardest to regain her composure.

"Baby, are you okay?" Terry asked again.

"That was Lawana."

"I know, you said it was her when you answered the phone. The movie is about to start so I came to get you. I could hear yelling as I approached the door. What's going on?"

"She said she saw you at some night club the other night."

"Yeah, I did see her. I didn't mention it because I didn't think it was that important. Actually, I saw her before she saw me. She was sitting at a table with that girl, Angela slamming down shots of Tequila. They were in their own world so I didn't bother them."

Carmen gave Terry a steely gaze as she searched for any sign of lying. Carmen could always tell when Terry was up to no good.

"Lawana said you were in the club hugged up with some woman."

"What?" Terry replied, looking appalled. "I was in there chillin' with my peeps. I wasn't hugged up with anyone."

Carmen didn't reply, she just continued her intense stare. Terry kicked the bullshit into overdrive.

"You know Lawana doesn't like me. If I even look like I'm doing somethin' wrong she's gonna come running to you. Besides, I told you I saw her before she saw me. Why would I mess with some woman in a crowded ass night club when there is a possibility that I could be seen?"

Carmen didn't know what to believe. She just placed her hands over her face, and leaned over, placing her head in her own lap. Her emotions took over. Her argument with Lawana was an intense one. The type of argument that can end a friendship.

"Terry, please tell me you didn't do what she said you did," Carmen mumbled while sobbing.

"No, baby," Terry pleaded. "She may have seen someone hugged up, but it wasn't me. She was obviously drunk. I'm not sayin' she's tryin' to break us up, but I can tell you that she's wrong. I didn't do it. I swear to you."

Terry reached down and pulled Carmen to her feet. The couple engaged in an embrace that lasted longer than Carmen's conversation with Lawana.

QJ was sitting next to his bedroom window which was located directly above the front porch. He heard everything. The sound of his mother crying sent the young lads dislike for Terry to another level.

The realization that Terry had driven a wedge between his mother and godmother was the final straw. It was at that moment that QJ made a vow to himself that he was going to get rid of Terry—by any means necessary.

Chapter 9

Quincy and Scoop had formed an alliance. They'd grown about as close as two homeless people could. Life in the streets mirrored that of prison. Latching on to someone you could trust was essential to ones survival.

For two straight days Scoop used his supermarket hook-up to get food for himself and Quincy. But, his scrounging hadn't been enough to get the money he needed to support his heroin habit. His body was talking to him. He needed a meal and a fix; and not necessarily in that order.

Now that Scoop's body was rendering him useless, it was Quincy's turn to be the hunter. He had to find enough food to feed his new buddy and get some money to help Scoop score. Time was ticking. Scoop was a junkie. If Quincy didn't help him out fast, some innocent jogger or senior citizen was going to get accosted.

"Look bruh, I know you ain't feelin' too good today," Quincy said, as he watched Scoop crouch near the tree, shaking and sweating as he battled withdrawal symptoms.

Scoop didn't reply; he just nodded.

"Well, I'm gonna go see what I can hustle up. Watch my basket. Inside that brown bag underneath the basket are some of those chips you got for us the other day. Go ahead and eat that."

"How long you gonna take?" asked Scoop.

Quincy grabbed the last empty garbage bag he had tied to the side of his shopping cart. He then pulled out a two-foot-long stick from his cart. The stick had a long rusty nail sticking out of one end of it. Since his encounter with Bookie he kept the stick close at hand. It served as both protection and a great tool for picking up soda cans. He'd become rather proficient at poking the nail in cans that were out of his reach.

"I don't know, bruh," Quincy replied, and then rubbed his rugged face. "Give me a few hours. I know where I can go, but it's gonna take a few hours for me to get there, hustle up somethin', and then get back."

Monday mornings were hectic. Carmen had an important meeting to attend so she left the house a little earlier than usual. QJ was happy to see his mother leave so early, that just meant he could do his own thing without being caught.

Rather than going to school like the other kids on his block, he ditched; opting to spend the bulk of his day in the projects shooting dice.

Weekday dice games in the projects, between nine o'clock in the morning and noon were the best to attend because they were least likely to get robbed. Most of the stick-up kids were nowhere to be found because they were plotting their nighttime armed robberies during the day. Rarely did the police do daytime drive-bys in the projects; therefore, getting picked up for truancy was the least concern for a wayward kid like QJ.

Money making was the focus, and on this particular day, QJ made a killing. He'd hustled some old timers out of nearly two hundred dollars. One crack head put up his son's Play Station console as collateral. When QJ won that he turned around and sold the console to one of the other gamblers for fifty cents on the dollar. He entered the dice game with $15 and walked away with nearly $250.

With a pocket full of cash, QJ prepared to meet his new girlfriend, Tia, on Canal Street. Tia was an Uptown cutie from a well-to-do family. Her parents were both doctors and owned a huge two story home a block off of St. Charles Avenue in the Garden District.

Tia was a student at the prestigious Catholic, all-girl Cabrini High School, located in Uptown New Orleans. It catered to the upper middle class African-American community. Because the African-American community is notoriously guilty of practicing elitism within its ranks, private school's like Cabrini served as the foundation for parents to mold their daughters into snobs and pretentious divas that qualified potential male mates based on their family's financial status, the texture of his hair, and skin tone.

A lighter skin tone was often the first criteria for a mate. The brown paper bag test was a barometer for companionship in the New Orleans African-American community—meaning that a potential mate could not be darker than said bag.

The irony of it all is that often times the girls being forced to attend schools like Cabrini spend most of their time devising plans to rebel against this forced separatist movement. Due to external pressures, they eventually conform to the status quo, but not until they've at least taken a bite of the forbidden fruit—a brotha from the hood.

QJ and his band of ragamuffins would be considered the poster children for the aforementioned forbidden fruit. He had a skin tone that was much too dark to ever enable him to pass the brown paper bag test. His tight fade couldn't hide the coarse texture of his nappy hair—a definite threat to sully the gene pool of the wavy haired elite. He was the product of a single parent household; a clear indication that he couldn't afford to properly escort a private school girl to her debutant ball or provide the type of bragging rights her parents needed to impress their friends.

QJ's incompatibilities didn't stop there. He didn't attend any of the elitist Catholic all-boy schools in the city: Jesuit, Brother Martin, or St. Augustine. Nope, QJ was a public school reject, struggling to stay afloat at one of the city's reform schools. Tia's parents would need psychiatric counseling if they knew their only daughter was dating such a boy.

Combine all of this outwardly discordance with the reality that QJ had the manners of a barbarian and the attitude to match; it's no surprise that he and Tia only rendezvoused on crowded Canal Street. Tia may have been curious, but she wasn't stupid. Bringing someone like QJ home would guarantee she'd be grounded for the entire school year.

Canal Street served as the perfect spot to meet because it was far from her St. Charles neighborhood. Downtown New Orleans is filled with tourists; white collar workers and women desperate to get back to their suburban neighborhoods; and blue collar workers catching connecting bus lines to their impoverished communities.

The odds of Tia being seen by some of her family members, most of whom wouldn't be caught dead shopping downtown, was nearly non-existent.

Always looking for a way to impress his high maintenance mate, QJ intended on using his winnings to buy Tia a pair of sneakers she'd been admiring. Tia beamed with pride as she strutted into the shoe store with her thug mate; making sure she waved at a few of her Cabrini classmates who were in the store perpetrating the same fraud with their outcast boyfriends. Knowing his reputation was at stake, QJ wasted no time displaying his wad of cash.

QJ eagerly stepped up to the cash register and paid the $60 for Tia's shoes. The cashier winked and smirked. The gesture served as a sign of approval—a silent high five from one poor black boy to another.

Although the caste system is traditionally associated with India, African-American's know that the concept is practiced every day within the community. The wealthy tend to mingle with their own kind, and the poor maneuver amongst their own ranks; linking up with an off limits dime piece like Tia was a source of pride amongst social outcast like QJ and the cashier.

QJ and Tia left the store grinning. The young couple strolled hand-in-hand down busy Canal Street without a care in the world. Canal Street was its busiest on the weekday between the four and six o'clock evening hours. School-aged students congregated in front of the old Joy and Sanger Theatres flirting, shooting dice, and sightseeing.

QJ and Tia hadn't been dating long. They'd met a month earlier on the bus, and hit it off immediately. Within weeks they could be seen canoodling, swapping spit, and engaging in the types of public displays of affection that would make any responsible parent want to snatch them both up by their collars.

"I gotta get home. Walk with me down to the corner so I can catch the next street car," said Tia, as she gazed into QJ's eyes like he was the most fascinating person she'd ever met.

"Fo sho," QJ replied, seemingly oblivious to the spell he'd cast over his naïve companion.

The couple interlocked fingers and walked towards the nearest street car stand. As they passed in front of McDonald's a group of boys stood outside smoking cigarettes, street vendors tried to hustle vials of knock-off cologne and perfume, and homeless men stood near waiting for one of those teenagers to discard a partially smoked cigarette.

"QJ!" someone shouted.

"Someone called you," said Tia.

"I don't know those dudes," QJ replied, hesitant to turnaround. QJ figured if he didn't look back it would reduce the possibility of him seeing some guy he'd fought previously. Bookie and Tweety weren't around to help. Engaging in an unsettled beef wasn't in his best interest.

"I don't think it was any of them that called you."

"What?" QJ replied.

"I think it was that homeless man over there."

QJ finally turned around to see whom Tia was referring too. Staring right at him was his father Quincy. Quincy wasn't looking much better than he looked the first time QJ saw him under the bridge. He was still wearing that tattered and dingy overcoat. That same dirty knit cap was propped on his head, and his shoes still looked like they'd been soaked in a vat of mud.

The only difference this time was Quincy wasn't pushing his rickety shopping cart. On this hot and humid day he was carrying a huge clear garbage bag and sifting through garbage cans. The bag was half filled with crushed soda cans—each can symbolizing the pendulum that swung dangerously from starvation and at least one hot meal for a homeless person.

Quincy waved enthusiastically at his son. The type of wave a father engages in when he's trying to get his child's attention at a commencement ceremony or some other crowded event where detection could be obscured.

"QJ, do you know him?"

"Who?"

"That homeless man over there."

Awwh shit. Of all the places for him to be, he would be down here today. I told him to stay away from this part of town. Bookie and Tweety are always hanging out down here. If they see him they're gonna hurt him.

And just my luck, he would call out my name on this day. I told Tia my daddy was dead. If I acknowledge him she's gonna start asking me all types of questions. Who is he? How do you know him? Questions I don't feel like dealing with.

Man, why is he down here on this busy street collecting cans? And why is he wearing that dirty ass coat? I swear if this nigga embarrasses me I'm gonna fuck him up, myself.

"Umm, I don't know him."

"Well, he obviously knows you. He's calling your name and waving at you."

"Umm, I think I may have met him once. I think I gave him a dollar or something. He ain't nothin' but some beggin'-ass homeless dude," QJ said, gently tugging on Tia's hand in an attempt to prompt her to ignore Quincy and keep walking.

Despite the pretentiousness of her parents, Tia was a kind girl. Slipping homeless people a few dollars or buying a homeless person a meal was a routine of hers. QJ was too busy being embarrassed to recognize that a kind gesture towards Quincy would have scored him major coochie points with Tia.

"Baby, you have a pocket full of money. You should give him a few dollars. Maybe he could stop digging in the trash cans."

"A few dollars ain't gonna help him," QJ replied, pretending to look down the street for the next street car. "He'll probably be back down here again tomorrow doing the same thing."

"That's true, but at least you would have helped him out today."

Man if I stop and talk to this dude he's gonna say something letting Tia know he's my dad. As hot as it is out here he's probably funky and sweaty. Fuck that, I ain't about to get exposed like that.

"C'mon Tia, here comes the street car. If we don't hurry up you're gonna miss it. The next one won't come by for another twenty minutes. You're already gonna have to explain to your pops where you've been."

Tia looked down at her wrist watch. "Yeah, you're right. Even if I catch this one I'll be lucky to make it home before six."

"That's what I'm tryin' to tell you. I don't want you to get punished. I'll come back and give that dude some cash."

"You promise?"

"Fo sho," QJ replied, and proceeded to flag down the driver.

Once he saw to it that Tia was on the street car and far enough away that she couldn't see him, QJ walked away from the tracks. He turned and looked back at Quincy. Much to his chagrin, Quincy was still standing there looking at him.

I wish he would just get lost. Why he gotta be hounding me out in public like this? He looks like a damn stalker or something.

Quincy waved once more at his son. The exuberance displayed in his previous wave was replaced with the type of wave that accompanies dashed hopes. The dejected look on his face only magnified his helpless disposition. He looked like a child waving goodbye to his lone friend at the end of summer camp.

QJ didn't reciprocate. In fact, he shook his head in disgust before he turned and walked across the street, heading towards the French Quarters. Quincy couldn't hide his embarrassment. He turned and walked in the other direction. If he could climb inside of the trash bag he held, he would have. Instead, he put his head down and continued his search for discarded cans.

It was dinner time. The sting of being dismissed by his only child would have to take a back seat. Quincy had more pressing issues to deal with like getting dinner so he could get back to Scoop, and his shopping cart.

Quincy managed to hustle up enough money to buy a few hamburgers from a nearby McDonald's. Purchasing drinks to wash them down was a luxury that would have eaten into the days profits, so he didn't bother.

I hope Scoop hasn't lost his mind by now. He was in bad shape earlier. I wouldn't be surprised if he'd held up a liquor store – that drug monkey was heavy on his back.

As Quincy approached the park he could see people running frantically toward the area Scoop jokingly referred to as his Living Room. Police were hovering around urging onlookers to keep moving. An ambulance was parked on the grass and EMT's were retrieving equipment from the rear of the vehicle.

Quincy knew something real bad had happened. He ran as fast as he could to the park, trying not to drop the bag of cold hamburgers.

"What's going on?" he asked.

"Stay back!," replied the police officer and gestured for Quincy to go away.

"Did something happen to Scoop?"

"Who?" asked the officer.

"Scoop. The homeless man that was over there."

"You know that guy?"

"Yeah, he's my friend," Quincy replied. When he saw the EMT's pull out a dark body bag his heart started to beat faster. They were standing near the shrubs where Scoop slept.

The police officer turned and walked over to another police officer. Quincy couldn't hear what they were saying, but he could tell by the way they kept looking back at him, they were discussing the fact that he asked about Scoop.

Before the officer could walk back over to Quincy, one of the EMT's walked past.

"Hey, man. What's going on with my friend? Is he okay?"

The EMT looked at Quincy and shook his head. "You know him?"

"Yeah, he's my friend."

"He's dead," the guy replied nonchalantly.

"Dead! What do you mean he's dead?"

"Mister, your friend is dead."

"What happened?"

"Asphyxiation."

"Asphyxiation?"

"Yes," replied the EMT, looking like he was frustrated by Quincy's question. "Apparently he was lying in his sleeping bag and choked to death on his own vomit."

As the EMT walked away, the police officer approached with a small note pad in his hand. Quincy was in a daze. Everything seemed to be happening so fast. The image of them placing Scoop's body in that body bag sent chills down his spine.

"Sir."

Quincy could hear the officer, but he was too stunned to reply.

"Sir," said the officer in a more assertive tone. "You said you knew the deceased? What was his name?"

"Sedrick... his name is Sedrick Bowe. People called him Scoop."

The officer started jotting notes on his pad. He didn't look up at Quincy when he started asking more questions. "Does he have any family?"

"No."

"You don't know anyone we can contact?"

The EMT's walked past pushing the gurney with Scoop's long body in that black bag. They were laughing about something. Their lack of interest was obvious. As far as they were concerned, Scoop was just another homeless man that had died on the streets. But, he was much more than that. They didn't know how remarkable an athlete he used to be. They didn't know how wise he was. They didn't know how much of an impact he'd had on Quincy during the short time they'd spent together.

"What the fuck are y'all laughing at?" Quincy shouted. "Y'all think this is funny? That was a man... a real man!"

"Calm down sir," said the officer.

"Where are they taking him?"

"To the morgue."

"What's going to happen to him?"

"I don't know sir. That ain't my job," replied the officer dismissively as he closed his note pad and signaled to the other officer that it was time to go.

Quincy stood there silently as he watched the ambulance driver carefully back the vehicle off of the grass and into the streets. As the ambulance sped away the police officers followed. The officer who'd questioned him was in the passenger seat. The man looked at Quincy and shook his head. Quincy couldn't tell if it was a look of pity or disgust.

Quincy walked over to the bench where he and Scoop had many of their discussions about life. He sat down and looked at the bag of hamburgers. His pallet was numb. He'd never felt so alone in his life. Scoop was his only friend. The only person he could talk to and not fear being judged.

Quincy sat the bag on the bench and noticed marks on the fading paint. The bench was used for multiple purposes. It was their sofa bed. It was the office where they held counseling sessions. Those marks signified how the bench was also used as a scoreboard for their chess matches. The letters S and Q were etched in the wood. There were six lines under the letter Q, none under the letter S. At the rate

Scoop was learning to play the game, it was only a matter of time before there would be lines under that S. If only Scoop could have hung in there a little longer.

Quincy needed a smoke like never before. He reached into his pants pocket to retrieve a cigarette and his matches, but he pulled out something else. It was the counselor's business card. It was wrinkled and stained, but the contact information on it was still legible.

Quincy looked over at the area where Scoop last slept, and then stared at the card for a few moments. His frown slowly turned into a smile. He smiled because even though his lone friend had passed away, Scoop was still giving advice.

Quincy rubbed his thumb across the raised letters on the card, and silently started talking to his friend. *I hear you Scoop. I hear you loud and clear. You don't have a reason to get cleaned up... but I do. It's time for me to be the coach my son needs.*

Chapter 10

Three days passed before Quincy was comfortable sitting on the bench Scoop referred to as his living room sofa. The park didn't seem the same since Scoop was gone. New homeless people seemed to be snooping around more, trying to weasel their way into Quincy's territory. The breeze didn't blow as blissfully. The sounds that signaled there was life in the area had dissipated. It was like Scoop's passing had zapped all of the energy from the place.

The thought of relocating to another area was heavy on Quincy's mind. As he searched through his basket for the bag that contained his eating utensils, he heard a familiar voice from behind—it was QJ's.

"I'm surprised you're not chillin' with your boy," said QJ.

Quincy paused, but didn't turn around. "What brings you around here? You didn't want to acknowledge me the other day when I saw you on Canal Street."

"So," QJ replied. "You didn't acknowledge me for ten years. I know you ain't trippin because I didn't come over and talk to you."

Quincy paused again. QJ was definitely his son. That razor sharp tongue and quick-witted remark was a definite giveaway.

"Touché," Quincy replied, and turned around.

"Yeah, I know I made a good point," said QJ in a cocky tone; proudly acknowledging that he fully understood the term.

They both sat on the bench. There was a few seconds of awkward silence before QJ decided to break the ice.

"So where is your homeboy?" asked QJ, as he turned around looking for Scoop.

"He's not here."

"So where is he? Out begging for money?"

Quincy gave his son a stern look. The kind of look a father gives his child when the child has crossed that invisible line that separates a child's place from an adult's.

"He's dead."

QJ wasn't expecting that announcement. He was visibly embarrassed and ashamed that he'd mocked a deceased man.

"Oh, my bad. I didn't know."

Quincy pulled out a cigarette. "So what made you come out this way? All of a sudden you want to talk to your old man."

"I was just checkin' on you," QJ replied. "You looked like you were in a bad state the other day so I brought you some stuff."

QJ gave Quincy a plastic bag full of toiletries: soap, toothpaste, toothbrush, mouthwash, and other stuff. Quincy was pleasantly surprised.

"Thanks, son," he said with a smile.

QJ cringed when he heard Quincy refer to him as son. "Say, dog. Let's not go there with that *son* stuff. I mean seriously, I don't know you like that and you don't really know me. Let's just keep it simple. You call me QJ and I'll call you Quincy."

"Fair enough," Quincy replied, clearly disturbed by QJ's remarks. "So, who was she?"

"Who?"

"The little cutie you were with on Canal Street."

"Oh, that's nobody."

"Must have been somebody. Y'all were all hugged up," Quincy said, and then smirked.

"Hugged up? Man get outta here with that. That's just my little boo. Her name is Tia."

"I saw she had on one of those Private school uniforms. Where does she live?"

"She lives off of St. Charles."

"Hmmm... one of those prissy Uptown girls."

"Yeah, she's from Uptown, but she ain't all stuck up like most of those chicks."

"Let me guess—she likes that thug in you. Her family doesn't know she's seeing you because if they did she would be forbidden from hanging out with you. Y'all meet up on Canal Street after school and hang out until it's time for her to go home."

QJ was surprised at how well his dad had summed up his relationship with Tia.

"How'd you know all that?"

"Son... I mean, QJ. I've been there and done that. The clowns may have changed, but the circus remains the same."

Quincy could tell from the look on QJ's face that he was struggling to decipher the metaphor so he translated it for him.

"All I'm sayin' is that it's the same type of situation that existed when I was your age. It may have been years ago, but the situation is the same. The rich girl likes the poor boy; the rich girls family hates it; the rich girl and poor boy sneak around until the girl's family finds out.

"What you need to be ready for is the day her family tells her she can't see you anymore. I'm just sayin'—protect your heart, man."

"Yeah, I hear you, but I ain't worried about that. Even if her people do find out, they can't stop this. I got this on lock."

Quincy looked over at his son. If their relationship had been closer he probably would have slapped the boy upside his head. The boy was too cocky to understand how foolish he sounded.

"So, you got it on lock?" asked Quincy sarcastically. "Are y'all having sex?"

QJ was taken aback by his dad's question. His mother had also asked him about his sex life, but he usually ignored her attempts to have a discussion about the birds and the bees.

"What?"

"Did I stutter? Are you and that girl having sex?"

"Yeah, I hit it once," QJ replied flippantly.

"Why?"

"What?"

"Why did you hit it?" asked Quincy as he stared deeply into his son's eyes.

"Man, you trippin'," QJ replied nervously. Although his mother had asked him similar questions about his relationship with Tia, for some reason, the question seemed more intimidating when it came from Quincy.

"I may be trippin', but you didn't answer the question," Quincy replied, still staring at his son. "You have a slick comment about everything else, but you can't answer a one word question."

"I can answer it."

"Okay, I'm listenin'. Why did you feel the need to *hit it*? You think that makes you a man?"

"Man get outta here with that. So what, you're a shrink or somethin'?"

"Nope. I'm just a man—who happens to be your father and who asked you a simple question. You know why it's taking you so long to answer that one word question?"

"Since you have all the answers, why don't you tell me," QJ replied, totally incapable of hiding his immaturity.

"You don't have an answer because there is no good answer to that question for a boy your age. You and I both know you shouldn't be having sex at all. The fact that you can't answer that question is proof."

Quincy took a few puffs on his cigarette and continued, "Let me ask you this. When you *hit it* that one time, did you use protection?"

"Yeah, man. I keep rubbers on me," the boy replied mannishly.

Quincy looked at QJ and then shook his head. He was clearly disappointed with the boy, but knew that he couldn't let it show because he was part to blame. His son was lost.

As Quincy looked at QJ, he reflected on a recorded impromptu speech he'd once heard that was given by Stokley Carmichael, the former Black Panther. The speech had been recorded while Stokley made a brief appearance at an event in New York in the late 1980's. Stokley said, "To be ignorant is bad, but to display arrogance within your ignorance is dangerous."

QJ was not only ignorant; the boy was filled with arrogance. He had teenage parent written all over him. Quincy wondered whether it was his place to intervene or should he keep his mouth shut?

Suddenly, Stokley's voice left Quincy's psyche and was replaced by the voice of his deceased friend Scoop, *When he comes back here lookin' for you again, are you gonna be the coach he needs or are you gonna drop the ball again?*

It was at that moment, Quincy decided to attempt to play coach, in spite of the circumstances.

"Look QJ, I know you don't wanna hear this, but I'm gonna say it anyway. You don't wanna ruin your life. If you are having sex with that little girl — or any little girl for that matter — stop it. You need to be focused on your school work right now.

"The last thing you need right now is to mess up and get some girl pregnant. I don't care if you have rubbers on you at all times, the only way to guarantee you don't become another teenage daddy is to abstain from sex."

That bewildered look engulfed QJ's face again. This time, Quincy didn't find it humorous.

"I mean avoid having sex. To abstain means to refrain from doing something, QJ. The fact that you aren't familiar with a simple word like that just proves my point. You are around here playing *grown folks* games and you aren't even familiar with the simplest *grown folk* words."

Quincy's tone was admonishing. For that moment he ignored the fact that he hadn't honored his responsibilities up to that point. The paternal instincts took over. He chastised the boy in a way that was both unexpected and long overdue.

Just because a remark is appropriate doesn't mean it will be well received. QJ sat quietly for a moment as he processed the tongue lashing he'd just received. He had mixed emotions. A part of him wanted to concede to his father's authority, but there was that other side of him; that untamed side that wasn't trying to hear what Quincy had to say.

"Man, I didn't come here to hear a speech," QJ replied in a defensive tone, which was accompanied by the applicable body language. "You haven't acknowledged me in a decade, and now you wanna give speeches and shit."

"Boy, you need to change your tone," Quincy said and grabbed QJ's forearm.

"Man, get your damn hands off of me! You ain't got no pull here! What makes you think you can just spit some advice my way and I'm just gonna run with it? This ain't the Cosby Show, dog. You ain't Dr. Huxstable."

"No, I'm not. But I'm your father and you're my son. I'm just trying to keep you from…"

"What? Keep me from becoming a daddy and then abandoning my child the same way you left me? You wanna teach me how to avoid being a deadbeat father like you?"

Quincy sat quietly and looked into the far distance as his only child stood there berating him. There was something wrong with this picture. He was the father. QJ was the son. So why was he being made to feel like the child? At what point was he authorized to put this angry boy in his place?

"Go ahead and say *touché* to that," QJ mocked. "Oh, now you wanna be quiet."

QJ looked up the street and saw the bus coming. He then looked at Quincy and started shaking his head. He pitied his father.

"Man, how you gonna preach to me and you don't even have your own shit together? When you get your shit straight then I will listen to one of your lectures."

QJ turned and started walking towards the bus stop. Quincy didn't bother stopping him; he was too busy licking his wounds from the tongue lashing he'd just taken.

He wondered if trying to be a coach to QJ was even worth the effort. QJ was set in his ways. The boy hadn't received any male guidance during the years he needed it the most. Quincy was ready to abandon the task, but he continued to hear Scoops voice, *He isn't gonna just change the way he's livin', and start listening to you. You're gonna have to put in some work.*

"Yeah, yeah, I hear you Scoop," Quincy mumbled. "I gotta put in some work. I guess it's time for me to get my shit together."

Chapter 11

The sprawling church parking lot had only three cars parked in it. Quincy paused for a second and contemplated walking away. He even wondered if he had the right church. There was a window on the far right side of the building. The blinds were open and he could see someone moving back and forth inside. Still, he was hesitant to go.

Quincy quickly became discouraged. He tried to talk himself out of this life changing decision. *Man, this is a waste of time. No one is here. It doesn't look like there are any meetings going on here.*

He was about to turn and walk away, but paused when he saw an SUV pull up and enter the lot. The paint job and large shiny rims made it look like it belonged to a drug dealer—not a church-going person.

Quincy watched closely as a tall black man exited the vehicle. The first thing he noticed were the huge diamond stud ear rings the guy was wearing. They shined as bright as the rims on his car. It had been years since Quincy had been around a church. His memory was somewhat cloudy, but he didn't recall preachers and deacons driving fancy cars and having flashy clothes, looking like they were on their way to the nightclub.

Once he was able to pry his eyes away from the man's material possessions, Quincy realized that the guy walking his way was Terrance Lock, the man who'd approached him at the park.

"I see you made it," Terrance said, as he stuck out his hand.

"Uhh, yeah. I wasn't doing anything so I figured I'd pass by," Quincy replied. His words were staggered and reflective of his nervous state. He shook Terrance's hand and quickly shoved his own scruffy hands back inside his pocket.

"Well, I'm happy to see you are here. What's your first name again?"

"Quincy. My name is Quincy Washington."

"Quincy Washington," Terrance repeated in a low tone as he stared at Quincy. His look was peculiar, like Quincy's name had triggered some long lost thought.

"Yeah. What's up?"

"Nothing," Terrance replied. "My mind just drifted for a second."

"Is the meeting still happening tonight? This place looks deserted."

"Yes, the meeting starts in about fifteen minutes. We don't meet in the sanctuary; we meet over there," said Terrance, as he pointed at a small house painted a hideous lime green located directly across the street.

It was small, maybe about 1,200 square feet, but the grass was perfectly manicured and the house was very well kept.

"That's church property. It was bought for the sole purpose of holding our H.A.B.U. meetings."

"Oh, but it still doesn't look like anyone is there. I don't see any cars outside."

"That's because many of the brothas that attend the meeting don't have cars. Trust me, they are in there. They are walking just like you. But that's okay; our focus is on getting men like yourself back on your feet. We wanna help you get your spiritual, personal, and financial house in order, so you can afford a car."

"I hear you," Quincy mumbled, as he glanced over at Terrance's vehicle. "Looks like you already got your act together."

"I'm blessed, my brotha. I don't mind sayin' it out loud. Being able to afford that car is nice, but I get greater pleasure in knowing that my God is a provider and will take care of my *every* need — not just my material needs."

Quincy nodded in agreement as he followed Terrance into the small house. He didn't know what to expect. He didn't know what would be expected of him. He'd already told himself that he was leaving the first time someone tried to humiliate him. He wanted help, but he wasn't about to let anyone speak to him like he was irrelevant.

The shotgun style house didn't leave much room for maneuvering. As they entered through the front door, iron folding chairs were positioned in a row. Terrance had to walk past three rows of those iron chairs before he got to the podium. There were only three other homeless-looking men in attendance.

Quincy sat on the last row; the same way he did back in the days when he did occasionally make it to a Sunday morning service. The other men in the room didn't notice his presence. Two of the men appeared to be around his age. Quincy even recognized one of them as a guy he'd seen rummaging for meals in trash cans on Canal Street.

The guy Quincy recognized and one of the other attendees sat quietly with their heads down. They were both staring at the floor looking like they wanted to be somewhere else. The other guy in attendance was much older. He had a more distinguished look. He wore dark thin framed glasses and was clean shaven. He looked a lot like Malcolm X, during his years with the Nation of Islam.

The Malcolm X look alike was studying his bible. He paused long enough to glance at Quincy, offer a warm smile and head nod, before he continued reading.

Terrance walked to the kitchen — which could be clearly seen from where Quincy sat — and starting talking to another tall gentleman who must have entered the building from the back entrance. Quincy figured he was probably a deacon because his conservative appearance seemed to fit the stereotypical image of a religious man.

The two of them walked back into the living room area. Terrance stopped at the podium, and the other man sat down on one of the chairs on the front row.

"Okay, it doesn't appear that we're gonna have anyone else joining us tonight," said Terrance, looking like a pastor at the pulpit as he looked upon the small crowd. "I'd like to start this meeting with a prayer. Please bow your heads."

Like the other men, Quincy's head was lowered, but he did sneak a peak at the rest of the men. He felt like he was attending a church service.

Terrance started, "Heavenly Father, we would like to start by thanking You for the gift of life, and Your unwavering willingness to bless and protect us in spite of our faults."

"Yes, Lord," said the tall man Terrance was talking to earlier.

"Yes, yes, yes," said the Malcolm X look alike.

Their spontaneous outburst moved Quincy to keep his one eye open during the entire prayer. He wasn't sure if he needed to keep an eye on everyone, but he wanted to be alert and ready to run in the event someone should try to douse him with holy water or something.

Terrance continued, "Father we ask that you guide tonight's discussion. We ask that you touch the hearts of the brothas in attendance this evening, and give them the sense of comfort and belonging that they seek. The fact that they are here tonight is proof that they are ready to make a change."

"Yes, Lord!" shouted the Malcolm X look alike.

The man shouted so loud that Quincy opened both eyes and looked around the room. The other men sat there with their heads bowed and acted like they didn't hear the man. Quincy wondered if the man was going to get the Holy Ghost.

"Father, today is the first day of their new lives. We come to You and humbly ask that You cast out those demons that have sidetracked them. Break those strongholds that keep them from achieving the heights You have set for them. In Jesus name we pray, Amen." Terrance concluded his prayer.

The other men said, "Amen." Quincy was the last to let the word flow from his mouth. He'd never been much on praying. He was unfamiliar with prayer protocol. In an effort to not look like a total dunce, he just did what the other men in the room did. When they raised their heads, he raised his head. When they stood up and started clapping, he did the same.

"Okay, gentleman, lets get started," said Terrance. "Tonight, Deacon Thomas will be sitting in on the session."

Quincy looked around and started silently sizing up everyone else in the room.

I figured he was a Deacon. He got that Deacon look about him. I wonder what Malcolm X's issue is. He looks like a Deacon too. I'll bet he was once an alcoholic. His face looks worn down like someone who has been drinking for many years.

I'll bet these two younger cats are trying to shake that rock. I can tell that one over on the left just got out of the penitentiary. He got all of those jail house tats on his forearms. Yeah, he's done a bid or two. He probably turned to drugs after he came home and couldn't get on his feet.

"I know who you all are, but I know some of you don't know each other. So that everyone will feel comfortable, I'd like for each of you to take a moment to introduce yourself and quickly let us know what your challenge is. Let's start with you, my brotha."

Terrance pointed at the Malcolm X look alike and gestured for him to stand up.

"My name is Nelson. I've been coming to these meetings for two months now to get back in touch with God. I was an alcoholic. I say *was* an alcoholic because I haven't had a sip of any type of alcohol in two months.

Honestly, I have no desire to go back to that lifestyle. I'm clean and sober and I intend to stay that way."

Everyone in the room applauded. The man had tears streaming down his face as he spoke. Quincy was moved by the sincerity in his words and mannerism.

The man with the jailhouse tattoos stood up, "My name in Bobby. Umm, this is my second meeting. Ummm…"

"Take your time, brotha," Terrance said, offering support to the young man.

"… I have a drug problem. I started smoking rocks when I got home from the Penitentiary. The mother of my kids moved away to another state with some other man, and I can't find her. I got so stressed that I just turned to cocaine. I just want to get cleaned up so I can go get my kids."

The man sat down and started looking at the floor again. He was clearly trying to fight back his tears. The other young man that sat near him stood up and spoke.

"My name is Stanley. This is my first time coming to this meeting. Ummm, I'm here because… I'm here because I'm gay and I don't wanna be gay anymore."

The young man's hands shook like he'd just pulled them out of a bucket of freezing cold water. The Deacon stood up and walked over to Stanley and hugged him. Everyone in the room started clapping so Quincy did the same.

He wants to stop being gay. I didn't know that was an option. I always thought people were born gay. How else can you explain pre-teen kids acting like sissies? If you're gay, you're just gay. If it was as simple as just stopping whenever you wanted to, I'm sure most gay people would stop.

"Yes, Lord," Terrance shouted. "We feel, You Father! Your presence is felt in here. I know you are going to save brotha Stanley from that stronghold."

Quincy watched as the young man started crying uncontrollably. He nearly collapsed right there. *Yeah, he gay.*

He damn near passed out just like a woman. I don't know if they're gonna be able to pray the sissy out of him.

Quincy was so busy sitting there passing judgment on his peers, he forgot he'd have to introduce himself – and be judged too.

"Okay, it's your turn," said Terrance, and looked right at Quincy.

"Who, me?" asked Quincy as he pointed at himself and looked around to see if there was anyone else Terrance could have been talking to.

"Yes, brotha. Stand up and introduce yourself."

Quincy took a deep breath, stood up, cleared his throat, and started to speak.

"Umm, my name is Quincy. I used to smoke crack, but I stopped that some time ago. Now, I'm just trying to stop drinking."

"Why?" asked Terrance.

"Excuse me?"

"Tell us what's motivating you."

"Well, I wanna get cleaned up for myself first, but I guess I'm tryin' to get cleaned up so I can be a father to my son."

The men in the room clapped – all except Bobby. Bobby looked back at Quincy and scratched his forehead. He was preparing to ask Quincy a question that would surely cause some tension.

"What do you mean you *guess* you're getting clean for your son?" asked Bobby.

Quincy paused for a moment and tried to decipher Bobby's tone. He looked around to see if any of the other men would chime in, but all eyes were on him.

"Yeah, I guess. I'm just tryin' to get myself together so I can deal with my son. The same way you are tryin' to get cleaned up to see about your kids," Quincy replied.

"Nah, dog. You ain't nothin' like me. I don't have to *guess* when it comes to my kids. I was locked up for eight years, and I never forgot about my kids. The only thing that got me through those long days in prison was the thought of my children needing me. I don't need to *guess* when it comes to them."

"Damn, dog. What's your problem?" Quincy asked, totally ignoring the fact they were in a church setting.

"I'm wonderin' why gettin' cleaned up for your kid's is an afterthought."

"It's kid. I only have one. A fifteen year old boy. I don't have a bunch of kids like you," said Quincy. His tone was extremely defensive. Not necessarily the type of tone you want to take with a dude that just got out of the pen.

Sensing things were getting a little tense, Terrance stepped from behind the podium and moved toward the chairs. He wanted to be prepared to step in between the two men should this disagreement escalated into fisticuffs.

Bobby stood up. "Yeah I have three kids, and I don't need to *guess* about any of them. You have one son and you make him sound like an after thought. Let me ask you this dude, have you ever been locked up and forced away from your son?"

"No," Quincy replied. He didn't want to answer, but he knew he had to answer to save face.

"Umm hmm. I can tell what type of brotha you are."

"What's that supposed to mean?"

"Nothin' man. Sit down."

"No finish your statement," said Quincy. "Since you think you got me figured out."

Bobby looked at Terrance to see if it was okay to speak freely. Terrance enjoyed this type of banter. He wasn't going to let it get out of control, but experience had taught him that this type of peer challenging amongst men can be extremely productive.

Nothing motivates a man like the thought of being seen as weak by his peers. Terrance looked at Bobby and gave him the permission to proceed by nodding his head and taking a step backwards.

"You got deadbeat written all over you."

"What? Nigga, you don't know me like that!" shouted Quincy, more embarrassed than offended.

The Deacon was scared they were about to start fighting. He looked like he wanted to jump out of the nearest window, and go running to find the Pastor.

Terrance reached and gently grabbed the sixty year old man's wrist, and winked at him. He realized that this was the Deacon's first time sitting in on a session; therefore, he wasn't accustomed to how heated the conversations could get at times. His touch went a long way towards settling the Deacon down.

"I didn't stutter. I said you look like a deadbeat!" Bobby barked back. "Let me ask you this. When was the last time you spent time with your son?"

Quincy started to refer to the discussion he had with QJ in the park the day before, but he knew that conversation didn't count. It wouldn't have happened if QJ hadn't tracked him down.

Quincy's pause was all Bobby needed to go in for the kill. "Just like I said, you're a deadbeat. I was locked up eight years, but I still spoke to my kids often and I wrote all three of them individual letters every week.

"Dudes like you make me sick. You have access to your kids and you don't even try to be in their lives. I know brothas in the pen that would kill to be able to see their children. The only reason I'm not with my kids is because their scandalous mama took them, and is hiding from me. She knows how I feel about my kids. She knows that's the only way she can hurt me.

"Man, I will kill a nigga…"

"Ummmm…" Terrance said, signaling to Bobby that he needed to change his language.

Bobby had forgotten he was in a religious environment. You can take a man out of the hood, but that doesn't mean you can take the hood out of him.

"My bad, brotha Terrance," said Bobby in an apologetic tone. "I just get ticked off when I see dudes like this."

"Man, you don't know what you're talkin' about," said Quincy, and then sat down. "How you gonna pass judgment on me?"

"I'm not passin' judgment on you and your addiction. Hell, I'm trying to shake my own addiction. As far as that's concerned we are all in the same boat.

"But it don't matter how hard it is for me to shake that crack, I don't ever have to be reminded about my kids and how important they are. Man, I can tell by the look on your face that you ain't doin' right by yours. I know a deadbeat dad when I see one. I don't respect dudes like you."

The room became silent. Bobby and Quincy stared at each other for a few seconds more. The stare down didn't cease until Bobby sat and turned towards Terrance.

The Deacon sighed aloud. Sweat beads had formed across his forehead. He sat back down and immediately started praying. What he was asking God to do was unknown, but it probably involved ending that meeting quicker than usual.

The other men in the room sat down and turned towards the podium. Terrance walked back behind the podium and one at a time made eye contact with every man in that room.

"That was an intense exchange between Bobby and Quincy. But you know what? It was a healthy exchange between two brothas that mean well. Being an active father is very important to Bobby. That's not to say it isn't important to Quincy, but it has a special meaning to Bobby because he was incarcerated and *couldn't* take care of his kids."

"Well maybe he shouldn't have gotten arrested," Quincy blurted out and stared at Bobby. "He's in here judgin' me. I can judge him too. If being an active father was so important to him, he should have stayed out of jail in the first place."

Terrance stood there quietly. His eyes darted back and forth from Quincy to Bobby. He knew that Quincy had made a valid point, but Terrance could tell by the nervous twitch in Bobby's leg that the point had not been deemed constructive criticism.

Bobby could dish out the barbs, but definitely wasn't prepared to handle the responses that came his way. Bobby never turned and looked at Quincy—a bad sign. Terrance then noticed that Bobby started clinching his fist—an even worse sign.

Terrance tried to change the subject, but he was a day late and a dollar short. Before he could complete another sentence, Bobby stood up and charged at Quincy.

Never one to run from a fight, Quincy flung a few of the chairs that were between him and his adversary out of the way. He threw up his hands and readied for battle.

The two men grabbed each other by the collars and prepared to wale until a clear winner could be determined. Fortunately for these two wayward souls, there was someone in the room who truly understood the value of H.A.B.U.—it was Nelson.

"Stop it!" shouted Nelson, in a voice that commanded respect. He looked at the two of them like he was their father. "Both of you should be ashamed of yourselves. This may not be the church, but this is the house of the Lord."

Quincy and Bobby stood there holding each other by the collar like two hockey players preparing to tussle. Quincy released his grip first. Moments later, Bobby did the same.

"You both are right," said Nelson. When he spoke, everyone in the room got quiet. Ironically, the glasses he wore, coupled with the respect he commanded at that moment, made him really seem like a young Malcolm X.

Quincy and Bobby both returned to their seats, but that didn't stop Nelson from speaking.

"Quincy, I don't know your story, but if you were capable of having a relationship with your son and you didn't then you were wrong," said Nelson, as he looked at Quincy. "And Bobby, Quincy is right. You can't criticize him for being a *deadbeat* as you put it, and then don't accept responsibility for the fact that you got yourself thrown into jail. Why were you sent to prison?"

"Armed robbery," Bobby mumbled.

"Armed robbery," Nelson repeated and shook his head in disgust. "Robbing someone and getting thrown into prison is a self-inflicted wound. You made *yourself* inaccessible to your kids. That's just as irresponsible as a man who is out here on the streets and deliberately avoids taking care of his children. One is no better than the other.

"The only reason I was able to make it through these two months here is because I relied on the men who were coming to these meetings with me. We were a support group for each other. Bobby you ain't no better than Quincy, and Quincy you ain't no better than Bobby.

"Y'all so busy lookin' for a reason to feel better than the next man that y'all are losin' sight of the real reason you are in here. The devil is a lie."

"Amen!" shouted the Deacon as he stood and lifted his hands. Terrance chuckled and shook his head as he watched the scary Deacon get his praise on.

Terrance used the Deacon's shout as an opportunity to interject. "Thank you, Brother Nelson. These brothas are just angry. Not at each other, but at themselves. You aren't each other's enemy. The enemy is the stronghold that has a grip of your thoughts—thoughts which dictate your actions. If we change the thoughts, we will in turn change the actions."

Terrance looked over at Bobby. Bobby knew what that look meant. He looked down at his feet for a moment, and then glanced over at Nelson. Nelson looked at Bobby and then nodded his head back towards Quincy; suggesting that Bobby should go back there.

Bobby stood up and walked towards Quincy like a school age kid being forced to apologize after a fight with a classmate. He looked at Quincy, who was still sitting in his seat, and extended his hand. Quincy looked around the room, and locked eyes with Nelson. Nelson nodded, signaling for Quincy to stand. Quincy followed the silent command of his elder, and stood. He looked directly into Bobby's eyes and then shook his hand.

"When you come through those doors we are family," said Nelson, in a deep base tone. He sounded like James Earl Jones. "There is no judgment here. If you can't offer advice or encouragement to your brother, then you need to be quiet or leave. The devil will not be allowed to destroy this—not while I'm here."

Bobby and Quincy returned to their seats. All in attendance focused their attention on the moderator, Terrance, as he returned to the podium. The H.A.B.U. session was about to begin… and Quincy's homeless and deadbeat lifestyle was about to end.

Chapter 12

Three Weeks Later

Things between Carmen and Terry had been somewhat tense since Lawana called a few weeks earlier and accused Terry of cheating. To go along with that tension was the fact that Carmen and QJ still hadn't spoken about Quincy.

Carmen was an emotional wreck. The three relationships that meant the most to her were crumbling right before her eyes. She felt overwhelmed and incapable of fixing them.

She didn't have the desire to discuss Quincy with QJ. She didn't have the courage to face the fact that Terry was a womanizer. And trying to get past the mean things she'd said to Lawana, seemed like a task that was going to take more energy than she could muster up at that time.

Carmen decided the best way to deal with the drama in her life was to just ignore it. She reasoned that things would eventually work out. She convinced herself that space and time were the perfect antidotes to the emotional poison that was choking her and eating away at her spirit. Unbeknownst to Carmen, her situation was about to get worse.

The scent of jambalaya dominated the house as she prepared Terry's dinner. The two of them had plans to watch movies and snuggle all night. Terry walked through her front door and slammed it so hard that the picture on the wall shook.

"What's wrong with you?" Carmen asked.

Terry was holding a letter in one hand and the envelope it came in, in the other hand.

"What's wrong with me? This is what's wrong with me. You ran up a $400 phone bill on that cell phone I loaned you!"

Carmen stood there with a confused look on her face. She grabbed the letter and read it carefully. Her mouth flew open. She was speechless as she sifted through the four page bill. There had to be one hundred phone calls on it. Many of them made after ten o'clock at night.

"This can't be right," she mumbled. "I only used the phone for a few days. I know I didn't make $400 worth of phone calls."

"Carmen, the proof is right there! Not only did you run up the phone bill, but you were making calls throughout the day—at the peek hours. Some of the calls were made at night when I wasn't around. What nigga have you been using my cell phone to call?"

"Terry, I can read. I see the total, but I'm telling you, I didn't do this. This bill must be wrong. I'm not seeing anyone else, and even if I was, I would never use your cell phone to call him."

"The bill ain't wrong! I spent an hour on the phone today arguing with the cell phone company. Those calls were made during the same time frame that I gave the phone to you."

Carmen thought carefully. She hated the phone, but she begrudgingly used the *dinosaur* until her Blackberry was ready to be picked up. The moment she got her phone back, she tossed Terry's phone in the top drawer of her dresser and forgot about it.

"Baby, I'm telling you, I didn't make these calls. I used that phone for two or three days—that's all. The moment I got my phone back I stopped using it."

"Umm hmm," Terry replied, clearly not believing a word Carmen was saying.

At that moment, the front door opened. QJ came in wearing a pair of baggy jeans that were hanging off of his butt, a back pack, and headphones. He didn't acknowledge Terry, which was no surprise. But, QJ walked towards the stairs and didn't even say hello to his mother.

"QJ!" Carmen called out.

QJ didn't look in her direction.

"QJ!" Carmen shouted again. "Take those damn head-phones off!"

The defiant teen turned and looked at his mother. He took his sweet time removing the headphones from his ears, and then let out a sigh that was so blatantly disrespectful it would have tested Martin Luther King's patience.

"What?"

"Did you use my cell phone?"

"What cell phone?"

"The phone I placed in my top drawer. Have you been using it?"

QJ rolled his eyes, and then turned and looked away. He started to take a step towards the staircase, but stopped when Terry spoke.

"Boy, your mama asked you a question. Did you use that cell phone she had in her drawer without her permission?"

"What if I did... it ain't none of your business."

"It is my business you little arrogant punk! That was my cell phone. I let your mama use it until she could get her cell phone fixed."

Terry walked closer to QJ. The tension in the room suddenly went up a notch. Sensing something bad was about to happen, Carmen tried to step in between QJ and Terry.

Terry continued. "And unlike your mama, I'm not gonna beg you for an answer to the question. I'm gonna ask you one more time. Did you use that phone without her permission?"

QJ contemplated his response. He knew he'd violated, but he wasn't about to concede an inch to Terry. The boy had a spirit that was so defiant; Mother Teresa would've had a hard time defending him. Besides, he'd intentionally misused the phone with the hopes that the outrageous bill would generate an argument that would send Terry packing. From the looks of it, QJ's plan was working perfectly.

"Yeah, I used it from time to time. What's the big deal?"

"What's the big deal? The big deal is that the bill is now over $400. Do you have the money to pay that? That's the big deal, stupid!"

"Whatever!" QJ shouted. "Fuck you! Your mama's stupid!"

QJ started to walk up the stairs, but he didn't get far. Terry reached around Carmen, and grabbed QJ's back pack.

"Don't turn your back on me you little punk! You wanna be a man, I'm gonna treat you like one," Terry shouted, and yanked QJ's back pack with so much force it caused the insolent boy to fall backwards.

QJ stumbled and landed on his back. His headphones were wrapped around his neck. He looked like a kid that had been running in his grandmother's backyard and forgot to duck when he ran towards the clothesline used to air dry the laundry.

Carmen screamed, and immediately tried to render aide to her son. Whether QJ deserved to be disciplined was irrelevant, her maternal instincts kicked in. Carmen's only thought at that moment was to defend her child.

She turned and looked at Terry and shouted, "Don't put your hands on my son again! Get back!"

When she turned to continue checking on QJ it was too late. The boy had already hopped up and was preparing for a fight. QJ tossed his mother to the side like a rag doll, and charged at Terry.

Terry hit QJ in his right eye with a stiff left jab, and then grabbed the boy's collar. The blow caught the teen off guard; stunning him to the point that his knees buckled.

A second blow was traveling at a rapid speed towards QJ's face, but it was intercepted—by Carmen's face. She attempted to protect her child from Terry's wrath and stepped in front of a blow that was meant to send a message to an out of control teenage boy. Instead, it sent a woman who'd never been punched before, stumbling backwards onto the staircase holding her mouth.

Everything seemed to be moving in slow motion to Carmen. This was like a scene from a *Lifetime* movie. Carmen never envisioned this type of drama in her life. During her short but eventful marriage to Quincy, he'd never struck her. Quincy would never attack her, and although Terry's blow was accidental, it symbolized a violent side Carmen never knew existed.

Seeing his mother crying and holding her mouth sent QJ into a rage. He kneeled next to his mother in an attempt to assess her condition. Carmen's hands were cupped over her mouth. Blood trickled from the gaps in her fingers. QJ struggled to pry Carmen's hands away from her mouth, while Terry stood a few feet away.

"Mama, let me see," QJ yelled.

Carmen squirmed on the floor with her hands over her mouth like she was trying to muffle the loudest laughter her shapely body could produce. Tears streamed down her cheeks and rested on top of her hands, mixing with the blood that had formed around her cupped hands to make the spillage look worse than it actually was.

"Mama, move your hand," QJ shouted again, as he finally managed to pull Carmen's hand away long enough to see the damage.

The left corners of Carmen's top and bottom lips were bleeding and had swollen like someone had latched onto them with a bicycle tire air pump, and pumped air non-stop.

QJ's hands started to shake as an unfamiliar anger surged through his body. Anger was too weak to define what QJ was feeling—this was an all out rage.

"Baby, I'm sorry," Terry whispered.

QJ looked up at Terry and backed away from his mother. Those who have been in a few fights know that it's not the loud outspoken person you should fear. It's the person who despite the level of provocation, seems to practice restraint.

Terry kneeled down to check on Carmen, but watched QJ like a black man getting a sneak peek at Nia Long in a thong. QJ returned the gesture by giving Terry a look that resembled a black man pissed that he'd missed his one chance to see Nia Long in that thong.

While Terry kneeled next to Carmen begging for forgiveness, QJ retreated to his bedroom. The boy walked slowly and quietly up the stairs and into his bedroom—his movement could have been described as zombie-like. When he re-emerged from his bedroom he was holding that same bat he'd pulled out a few weeks earlier.

He took his time coming back down the stairs; careful to not alert Terry to his cruel intentions. Terry was so caught up in trying to console Carmen that QJ's stealth approach went totally undetected.

"Baby, I'm so sorry," Terry said.

Carmen stared up at Terry with a look that resembled more disbelief than pain. The look in her tear-filled eyes said it all. She was in disbelief; astonished and even ashamed that she could fall so deeply and recklessly in love with someone who was capable of such brutality.

"Yo ass gonna be even sorrier when I'm finished with you," shouted QJ as he swung the silver, 32 inch, Easton aluminum baseball bat he'd had since he played for the nearby playground team when he was 12 years old.

The bat cut through the tension filled air like a swing from Barry Bonds. Terry looked up at the sound of QJ's voice, but it was too late—the beat down was underway.

The sound of the bat crashing against Terry's forearms, back, and legs was bloodcurdling. No special effects like the ones used in motion pictures. No words displayed overhead like *bang* or *pow* to symbolize the sound. Just loud thumps followed by barely indecipherable pleas for help being vociferated by the recipient.

Terry withdrew to a nearby corner and curled up for self preservation. QJ had wanted to inflict this type of pain on Terry for months. He'd often daydream about this beat down. Now the day had finally come, and he had a legitimate excuse—or so he thought.

Based on the moans spewing from Terry's lips, only one or two more blows were needed to ensure a 911 call. QJ panted heavily as he retracted that bat like a boy with homicide on his mind.

"QJ, stop!" Carmen shouted.

QJ was in a swinging motion when he heard his mother's voice. His pause was nothing more than admission that he'd heard her voice, it in no way was meant to imply that he would cancel the battering.

QJ looked at his mother and then took a step backwards and prepared to swing. His sole desire at that moment was to split Terry's head so that the contents would spill like a broken piñata.

"I said stop, QJ!" Carmen shouted again. And then lunged at QJ and grabbed the bat.

"Move, Mama," QJ urged.

"No, QJ! Stop!" Carmen shouted as she stood there grunting and wrestling with her protector for control of the bat.

QJ's grip was tight. So tight that Carmen had to go to the extreme to dislodge it from her son's grasp. QJ was stronger than her. She couldn't get the bat from him. She knew that if she released her end of the bat QJ was going to kill Terry.

The smack was loud. If the scene had been shown in slow motion, viewers would have seen QJ's left cheek jostle and shimmy like he was standing in a wind tunnel. Droplets of spit escaped his slightly parted lips and flew aimlessly in the air looking for some solid place to land.

QJ released the baseball bat and clutched his face. The blow stung, but his feelings were hurt more.

"Mama, what are you doing?"

"I told you to stop it, QJ!"

"Why are you slappin' *me*? I'm not the one who punched you!"

"I told you to give me the bat," Carmen shouted, in an indirect attempt to explain the reason she'd slapped her only child. "Go up to your room!"

"What?"

"You heard me. I said, go up to your room!"

Terry was still nestled in the corner. QJ looked at his mother with astonishment as he tried to process the chain of events. Terry hit QJ. Terry hit Carmen. QJ hit Terry. Carmen hit QJ. The sequence didn't make sense to him.

"Why are you hittin' *me*, Mama? Terry started all of this!"

"I said go to your room, QJ!"

QJ was shocked. Betrayed is probably a better way to describe how the boy was feeling. He looked at his mother and then at Terry before walking up the stairs. Carmen immediately went to Terry's aide.

"Are you okay, baby?"

"I didn't mean to hit you," Terry managed to mumble while crying. QJ had beaten Terry so badly that Terry's tough talk had been replaced with tears.

"I know, baby," Carmen replied, her total focus on consoling Terry.

Carmen was so consumed with consoling Terry that she was surprised to see QJ come back down the stairs a few minutes later. The boy was carrying a huge duffle bag. When he got to the bottom of the staircase he grabbed his book bag and headphones from off the floor.

"Where are you going, QJ?"

"I'm gettin' the hell outta here. It's clear to me who you're more concerned about. I'm going stay with Lawana."

"QJ, don't you leave this house!"

"Both of y'all can kiss my ass!" QJ shouted and stormed out of the front door—only breaking stride long enough to plant his size ten tennis shoe in the middle of Terry's car door.

Carmen stood still for a few seconds and then dropped to her knees. She sobbed openly as she tried to make sense of everything that had happened during the previous ten minutes—ten minutes that felt like ten hours.

The outpouring of tears and emotions lasted for nearly an hour. But the bawling wasn't only coming from Carmen. The entire time Carmen sat there crying her eyes out—Terry sat there crying too.

The shattering of glass could be heard throughout the entire house. The sound of flesh being smacked and beaten up resonated. Under the current tense climate and pre-existing circumstances, this could only mean one thing—Lawana was having wild, kinky, passionate, sex.

"C'mon you big, strong bastard!" she shouted, her hair strewn all over her head and in her face. "Fuck me like you mean it!"

Christopher was no little boy Lawana could just talk trash to without repercussions. He was a former NFL linebacker. He stood 6'4", and had a physique that suggested he still played football—even though his surgically repaired knees would beg to differ.

Christopher's muscles had muscles. His pecks looked like two tiny mountains. His abdominal muscles were so pronounced they looked like they'd been drawn on with a black Sharpie marker.

The thing Lawana enjoyed the most about Christopher was that he was a natural competitor; the type of man who was just as concerned about winning in bed as he was on the football field. Christopher would have rather cut off his own testicle than climax before Lawana. Lawana loved that quality.

"So, you wanna talk shit. You're gonna make me use this spatula on your ass," said Christopher, sweat beads streaming down his face and chest.

"Use that spatula you big, black fucker! Flip my ass if you think you're man enough!"

Christopher gladly obliged. He'd been pounding away at Lawana's vagina for fifteen minutes while she was perched on her dresser. Her head was hitting the mirror so hard it was a miracle it hadn't cracked. Her insistence on questioning his ability caused him to hit her with a move she wasn't expecting.

Christopher stepped away and removed his ten inches from Lawana's cave. With the strength of a wrestler he pulled Lawana off of the dresser and then turned her around. Lawana didn't fight him.

"Turn your ass around," Christopher ordered, and then pushed her head down on the dresser.

Lawana was dizzy. Her dizziness was compounded by the erotic stinging sensation that resulted from him smacking her soft ass with the spatula.

"You wanna test me? Raise your ass up!" he shouted, and then smacked Lawana's cheeks with the spatula again.

Carnal screams escaped Lawana's mouth. Her scalp was damp with perspiration as she watched her lover through the dresser mirror. Christopher tugged on her hair and cursed loudly as he punished her. He was stroking her like she owed him money and refused to pay.

The grimace on his face became uglier as he plunged deeper inside of her. Lawana's body invited this intrusion. She reached around and planted her fingernails in his ass cheek and pushed back harder. She watched him through the mirror. Her gaze was defiant. Her eyes were encouraging him to go deeper. Although the sweat beads that formed along her brow suggested that he may have already been deep enough. But that mouth... that mouth of Lawana's, spoke the truth. And during her passion filled sexual encounters, her mouth was brutally honest.

"That's all you got, you little punk?" she mocked, drool seeping out of the corner of her mouth.

Her taunts only heightened Christopher's testosterone level. His nipples became as hard as hers as he prepared to unleash his gusher inside of Lawana, and all over her sweaty back. The sight of Christopher preparing to climax and him spanking her with that spatula were the visual stimulants that drove Lawana to multiple orgasms.

Lawana placed her sweaty palms on the mirror as she and Christopher synchronized their orgasms. Little frost circles formed on the mirror as her panting became more pronounced, causing her lustful breaths to spew onto the mirror. The smacking sound of their hips was at an all-time high. The sound was so audible that she didn't hear the doorbell ring or the pounding on her front door.

While Lawana was in her bedroom getting her freak on, QJ was outside hoping she'd answer. He saw her car parked in the driveway so he knew she was home.

"Did you hear that?" asked Christopher.

"Hear what?" asked Lawana, struggling to control her breathing and clear the ringing sound in her ears.

"I think someone's knocking."

They both stood still and stopped panting long enough to hear the knocks.

"Shit!" Lawana shouted. "Who in the hell is that?"

"Maybe you should go and see."

Lawana begrudgingly backed away from her dresser. She chuckled at the sight of the broken picture frame and vase that lay on the floor.

"You're gonna replace my stuff," she said, and then grabbed her robe.

"I'll think about it," Christopher replied as he collapsed on the bed.

The pounding on her front door seemed louder once she regained her hearing.

"I'm coming… damn! Stop banging on my door. Who is it?"

"Lawana, it's me, QJ. I need to come in."

Shit! QJ hasn't been here in months. He would pop up over here today. "QJ? What's wrong, baby?"

"I need to come inside. I need somewhere to stay."

Shit, something bad must have happened. "Ummm, okay. Give me a second to put on some clothes; I just got out of the shower!"

Lawana ran back into her bedroom to alert Christopher.

"Umm, you gotta go."

"What?"

"Put on your clothes, you gotta go."

"Are you serious?"

"Yes, I am. My godson is here. Something has happened. I need you to get your stuff and leave. You can leave out the back door."

"Leave out the back door?"

"Look, Negro; stop asking questions. Grab your shit and leave out the back," said Lawana in an agitated tone, as she retrieved a t-shirt and jogging pants from her drawer.

She put on her clothes and returned to the front door. "QJ, are you still there, baby?"

"Yeah."

Lawana opened the door. She looked like a teenager who'd just been busted having sex by a relative. QJ wasn't sure what he'd walked in on, but he was wise enough to know his visit had come at an inopportune time.

"Umm, you want me to come back later?"

"No, no, baby. Come on in. I was just getting out of the shower. Come on in and sit down so we can talk," Lawana replied as she peeked down the hallway to see if she could see Christopher leaving out of the back door.

QJ plopped down on Lawana's soft sofa. He looked distraught. His shirt was torn at the collar. His eye looked swollen. A blind man could see that the boy had been beaten. Lawana's focus shifted away from her lover and to her godson.

"What happened, baby?"

Before QJ could answer, Christopher walked pass en route to the front door. His shirt was partially unbuttoned and his pants were loose—his belt dangling from the loops. Lawana wanted to crawl under the sofa.

"Oh, hey," she said nervously. "I thought you were gone."

"I'm leaving now," Christopher replied, determined to leave out of the house the same way he'd entered. "What's up, lil man."

"What's up," QJ replied.

Christopher exited the house without uttering another word. Lawana stared at the door long after it closed behind Christopher. She was too embarrassed to lock eyes with QJ.

"Taking a shower, huh," the boy wise cracked. "Wait a minute. Isn't that the dude from the restaurant? The big dark skinned dude that escorted us to the table. I thought you said he wasn't your type? And why is he carrying that spatula?"

Embarrassed and wishing she had the ability to snap her fingers and vanish, Lawana cleared her throat like she was about to make a speech. "Never mind that. What happened to you?"

QJ quickly refocused on the reason he'd come over unannounced. "I got into a fight with Terry."

"What?"

"Me and Terry had a fight."

"An argument or an actual fist fight?"

"Look at my face, Lawana. What do you think?"

"What happened, QJ?"

"That fool called me stupid!"

"What? Why?"

"Because I ran up the bill on a cell phone."

"What cell phone?"

"A few weeks ago Terry gave my mom a cell phone to use while hers was broken. I used it a few times and now the bill is $400."

"QJ, you had to have used the phone more than a *couple of times* to run up a $400 bill. How did the fight start?"

"Terry called me stupid. I said some things, and then we started scrapping."

"Where was your mother?"

"She was right there. She took Terry's side and hit me."

"What?"

"Yeah, she tried to make me go to my room. I just grabbed my stuff and left. Can I stay here with you?"

Lawana was like a mother-figure to QJ, but she wasn't looking for a permanent house guest. There was a reason she didn't have any kids — she loved her freedom. Being an everyday parent wasn't a lifestyle she'd ever desired.

"Umm, let's just take a deep breath and think about this."

"I don't need to think about it. I'm never going back to that house. Not while Terry is hanging out over there."

"Has Terry moved in?"

"Damn near. Everyday I see that truck in the driveway."

"Well, I can't deny, I'm not a fan of Terry either. You can stay here until we can figure all of this out," said Lawana, and then kissed QJ on the forehead. "You want something to drink?"

"What you got?"

"I got some bottled water, Coke, and some Kool-Aid."

"What kind of Kool-Aid? Red or purple?"

"Red or purple? Boy you just as ghetto as you wanna be," said Lawana and shook her head. "I have grape Kool-Aid."

"Yeah, I'll take some of that."

Lawana went into the kitchen to get the drink. She returned with a tall glass of Kool-Aid and a hand towel.

"Wipe your face. You're sweatin' like you just ran a marathon."

QJ took the towel and gulped the glass of kool-aid down within seconds.

"I have a confession," QJ said.

"What?"

"I ran up the minutes on that phone intentionally."

"What? Tell me you're lying."

QJ shrugged his shoulders and started laughing. "I'm gonna keep it real with you. I used the phone and ran up the bill because I was hoping it would piss off Terry enough to make them break up."

Lawana looked at QJ and then slapped him in the back of his head. "Boy, have you bumped your head? You shouldn't have done that. I know your mom can do better too, but misusing that phone wasn't a smart move."

"Tell me about it. I'm sitting over here and Terry is still there. I don't know what my mama sees in Terry."

"I can't argue with that," Lawana replied. "I've tried to talk to her, but she ain't tryin' to hear it."

"I know you've tried to talk to her. I overheard that phone conversation y'all had a few weeks ago. I know you busted Terry doing some dirt. My mama is sprung!"

"Yes, she is. Did the two of you ever talk about the situation involving your dad?"

"No. She was in the middle of having sex with Terry when I tried to talk to her."

"What?" Lawana shouted. "Never mind. I don't wanna know what you stumbled on."

The two of them sat quietly for a few minutes. QJ was reliving the fight. Lawana was pondering QJ's attempt to sabotage Carmen's relationship. She needed to open Carmen's eyes. But love is blind; it would take something or someone whom Carmen was invested in emotionally to pry her away from Terry.

"Have you seen your father since that encounter?"

QJ didn't reply right away. He looked away and contemplated his response.

"Yeah."

Lawana asked the question, but was still surprised by the answer. "When?"

"I've seen him a few times."

"Where?"

"He hangs out at Palmer Park in the 17th ward."

"That park that's on the corner of Carrollton Avenue and North Claiborne?"

"Yeah."

"How do you know that?"

"Because I told him to go over there. I knew my boys were plotting to shank him so I told him to go there so that they wouldn't find him."

"Well, have the two of you talked?"

"Yep. He told me everything?"

"What do you mean?"

"Just what I said. He told me everything that happened. He told me about the cruise Mama took with you. He told me when she came back she gave him the claps."

"He shouldn't have told you that."

"Why? He just gave me his side of the story. As much as I hate the way he handled his business with me, I can't hate on him for being pissed off. I would have been pissed too."

The usually outspoken Lawana sat there as quiet as a mouse—a personality change that didn't go unnoticed by her young house guest.

"How could you let that happen?" QJ asked.

"QJ, it's complicated. Your mama wasn't happy. She and your father were already having problems. Things happen sometimes."

QJ rolled his eyes and stood. He walked over to the large window and peered through the curtains. The sun was setting and the street lights were coming on.

"Well, I went to that park and talked to him a few times."

"Why?"

"I don't know. I guess I just wanted to get some questions answered. He gave me more info than you or my mama."

Lawana continued to sit there quietly. She never liked Quincy, but she knew that he was the one man whom Carmen had once loved unconditionally. Before alcohol and drugs changed him. It was at that very moment that a thought crossed her mind; something she wouldn't have ever contemplated before that day.

"QJ, I will admit that in hindsight maybe your mother should have handled things differently. Unfortunately, we can't change the past. All we can do is focus on the future. "

"Man, I don't have a future."

"What? Boy, don't talk like that."

"I'm serious. I don't have a daddy and it doesn't look like I have a mama, after today."

"QJ, your mama loves you. Sometimes things get heated and people say and do things they don't mean. I wasn't there so I can't comment on the fight. But, I know your mother loves you — more than she loves herself."

"Yeah, but she doesn't love me more than she loves Terry."

QJ's remark cut Lawana to her core. She could feel his pain. It was time for her to take action. Desperate times call for desperate measures.

While QJ was intruding on Lawana, Quincy was on his way to his second H.A.B.U. meeting. The first meeting had been intense, and rather uncomfortable. Nevertheless, he saw the intrinsic value in the group session. As much as he didn't want to attend, he knew it was the only way he'd be able to change his life.

As he approached the church parking lot he started to cross the street and walk over to the meeting site. He stopped when he saw Terrance coming up the street in his fancy SUV.

Terrance passed in front of Quincy and then parked in front of the church. He looked angry. So much so, Quincy was hesitant to speak.

"Hey, Terrance," Quincy finally blurted out as Terrance exited the vehicle.

"Hey," Terrance replied and gave a half-hearted wave.

The brotha was clearly in a foul mood. His hand was wrapped in a bandage, and he was limping. There was damage to his back fender and rear car door.

"Are you alright?" Quincy asked.

"Umm, yeah I'm okay," Terrance replied.

"Did you have an accident?" asked Quincy as he ran his hand along the dents in Terrance's door and fender.

"Umm, yeah," Terrance hesitantly replied.

"Oh," said Quincy, realizing that the man was in no mood for small talk. "So, are you coming to the meeting tonight?"

"No, I'm not. I got some personal stuff I need to take care of. Brother Nelson is going to facilitate tonight," Terrance replied and hastily walked into the church without saying good-bye.

Quincy dismissed the rude behavior of the normally courteous man. Realizing that Terrance's disposition had nothing to do with his journey to salvage his own life, Quincy made his way across the street, and went inside.

The nervous jitters that had seized control of his body before were dissipating. The fear of the unknown had been removed and replaced with the desire to change. Quincy was well on his way to recovery. He could feel it.

Upon entry into the house he was greeted by Brotha Nelson.

"Welcome, Brotha, Quincy," the humble man exclaimed and gave Quincy a firm handshake.

Quincy shook Nelson's hand and smiled. It's amazing the impact a firm handshake can have on men. It had been years since anyone had shook Quincy's hand with such zeal, and it injected a warmth in his spirit that one usually only gets while hearing a soul stirring sermon.

Amongst men, a man's handshake spoke volumes to Quincy. It was one of those subtleties about manhood that added credence to the theory that it took a man to teach a boy how to become a man. Quincy once believed the significance of this simple gesture must be taught from generation to generation.

He often thought the handshake between men could be the precursor to sealing an important deal or being a deal breaker. It was the male equivalent to small talk. A firm handshake said: I respect you; I welcome you; I'm not afraid of you; I don't think I'm better than you; I'm flawed just like you; I will defend you; I trust you; I believe in you; and most importantly, I'm here for you.

Nelson's handshake was deliberate. He intended to send a message to this two-time visitor. He wanted Quincy to know that all he needed to do was show the desire to change, and the brothas at H.A.B.U. would be there to help.

Nelson's greeting removed any lingering doubts Quincy' may have had about whether he was where he needed to be.

Rather than sit in the back of the room, Quincy sat in a seat on the front row. As he readied himself for the group discussion, someone tapped him on the shoulder.

"Welcome back, bruh," said Bobby, Quincy's adversary from the first meeting.

Quincy's frame of mind had changed since their last encounter, and so had Bobby's. Quincy stood and gave Bobby dap and in an effort to show Bobby that there were no hard feelings, he leaned in and wrapped his free arm around Bobby's back and gave him a thump. Bobby smiled and returned the gesture.

This was yet another gesture that spoke volumes to Quincy. Where as the firm handshake had its own language, he believed the way a black man shook another black man's hand took the greeting to another level.

During his many years on the street, he had plenty of time to reflect on the interactions of his people. He came to the conclusion that African-American's were known for improvisation. It showed in their music, the way they danced, and their style of dress. He knew they had a way of speaking without opening our mouths. The way black men shook hands was the equivalent of street slang—their way of speaking to each other.

Quincy witnessed that when meeting a total stranger, black men give the firm handshake. That's where their similarities with Caucasian men ended. If a black man was introduced to another man by a mutual friend, the handshake went from the traditional grip to the elaborate soul brotha grip. This gesture said—you're cool with me because you are hanging with my friend. But, when two black men wanted to send a message to each other that they were now friends, and not just passing acquaintances, the elaborate soul brotha shake was topped off with a chest-to-chest embrace, and an accompanying pat on the back with the free hand.

But, he knew that any black man would say that this gesture was necessary if peace between brothas was to ensue. Two black men that had supposedly squashed their *beef*, greeting each other with the *normal* handshake or head nod, still had unresolved issues with each other. They were powder kegs just waiting for someone to strike a match.

Bobby and Quincy had made peace with each other in their minds, but that greeting was affirmation to each other, and to the other men in the room.

The men sat and talked for the next forty minutes about various topics: self-respect, dedication, and prayer. Each person taking turns giving their feelings on their respective challenges. Nelson quarterbacked the show. Like a maestro he controlled the tempo; making sure every voice was heard. There was a positive synergy in the room that was indescribable.

Shortly before the meeting ended Nelson looked at each man, and asked him to explain how he was going to address the biggest challenge that had resulted from his respective challenge. Quincy had already confessed that his alcoholism had lead to his abandoning his son, so it was now time for him to begin formulating a plan on fixing the mess he'd created.

"Brotha Quincy, you've told us that you've been talking to your son. Since you lost ten years of life with your son, arguably his most impressionable years, how are you going to regain his trust so that you can start molding him into the proud black man he's supposed to be?"

Quincy sat quietly as he searched for an answer that didn't sound stupid. The room was silent and all eyes were on him.

"Ummm, ummm," he mumbled as he searched for an answer.

"Take your time, bruh," Bobby uttered, and gave a supportive wink.

"Ummm, I'm gonna be honest with you, Brotha Nelson. I don't know," Quincy shamefully replied.

Brotha Nelson smiled, and placed his elbows on the podium and leaned forward.

"I respect your answer. You didn't sit here trying to tell us what you thought we wanted to hear. Your answer was honest. That tells me you are ready to receive help. That's what H.A.B.U. is about. We are all here to help each other up."

Quincy shook his head to acknowledge that he did need help. He then leaned back in his chair and let out a loud sigh.

"I'm going to be honest with y'all. The few times I've seen my son it's been awkward. He acknowledges my presence, but he doesn't respect me. I can tell by the way he acts and talks to me. He treats me more like I'm one of his little buddies. There isn't that respect boys are supposed to give their fathers.

"Considering what I did to him, I can't say that I blame him. Honestly, I don't know how to overcome that. If y'all have any suggestions, I'm all ears."

The room remained silent. Brotha Nelson waited to see if any of the other men would offer any words of wisdom before he spoke. When it was clear to him that no advice was forthcoming, he chimed in.

"Let me ask you something, Brotha Quincy. When you and your son meet, does he come to see you or do you seek him out?"

"He comes to the park where I've been sleeping. He usually pops up from out of nowhere."

"That's good to know. That tells me that he desires a relationship. If he desires a relationship he will be more receptive to your instruction."

"You think?" asked Quincy.

"I don't just think my, brotha—I know," Nelson replied, with a confidant grin. "The signs of defiance that you described are the byproduct of juvenile machismo.

"Gentleman, we must always remember, we are black men. We descend from Kings. We were meant to rule. Our sons carry our genes. Most of the *beef* between these young brothas out here on these streets are the result of territory marking; one brotha trying to show the other that he's the biggest and toughest Alpha Male.

"We come from a culture where young men respect their elders—especially strong male figures." He looked back at Quincy. "If you think you're going to regain his trust by being nice and allowing him to disrespect you, either overtly or in subtle ways, you're sadly mistaken. The only way you will regain your son's trust and respect is by re-establishing your role.

"You are his father; therefore, as long as you are alive, you are the head Alpha Male in that family. You sit on the throne. He is meant to sit at your side."

All of the men in the room shook their heads as if Nelson's words had struck all of their sense of pride simultaneously.

Nelson continued, "Brotha Quincy, the next time you see your son and he does something rude or disrespectful, you correct him on the spot. Act as if you never walked out of his life. Talk to him as if you have a right to. You know why? Because you do have a right to talk to him assertively—you're his father."

Quincy stared at Nelson as if he was Jesus Christ speaking to him from the clouds. He hung on the wise man's every word. Even though he was receptive to Nelson's advice, he couldn't help but wonder how QJ would react to any form of discipline coming from a man who'd voluntarily abandoned his paternal responsibilities.

"Brotha Nelson," said Bobby, as he raised his hand asking for permission to speak like he was in Elementary School.

"What's on your mind, my brotha?"

"I hear what you're sayin, but these young kids out here today are rough. They don't accept discipline well."

"You're right, Brotha Bobby," Nelson replied, and then refocused his attention on Quincy. "Brotha Quincy, I'm here to tell you that the first time you correct your son he's going to become defensive. That's all a part of the process. It's not in his DNA to back down from someone he doesn't respect. But remember, you are trying to earn respect, and there is only one way to do that when dealing with any man, you have to take a stand.

"The first time he does something disrespectful in your presence, you look him directly in the eyes and let him know that the behavior is unacceptable and won't be tolerated. He is going to huff and puff, and may even walk away, but he'll be back. And when he returns, he will return minus that behavior he displayed in the previous encounter."

Those were Nelson's final remarks before he ended the meeting with a prayer. Quincy walked away with a sense of pride he hadn't felt in years. And although his destination was a park bench, all that talk about being descended from kings had him feeling like the Zulu King himself, Shaka Zulu. All he needed was a spear, chest plate, and nose ring to compliment his mood.

He was determined more than ever to get his life back on track and reconnect emotionally with his only child. A mighty task for sure, but one the newly crowned king was eager to take on.

Chapter 13

The dark storm clouds that seem to always hover over the city of New Orleans had once again taken up residence. The sky was gloomy and the streets were wet and slick from the annoying light rain that had been falling for hours. It was the type of day that made most people opt for comfortable clothes, made-for-television movies, and popcorn rather than shopping and perusing the city's many landmarks.

The St. Charles street car was parked in the center of the street preparing to turn around and make its way back through the Garden District. Joggers stuck to their routines and braved the elements as they focused on their pace and form rather than the possibility of being drenched by Mother Nature's tears.

Quincy looked like a jogger himself as he ran across the busy avenue. He'd just come from the back of the grocery store getting a sandwich from the young lady Scoop had turned him on to.

As he made his way to his home, he heard someone calling his name.

"Quincy!"

Quincy glanced quickly to see the source, but never broke stride as he headed towards his tree.

"Quincy!" someone called again.

Quincy continued towards his tree. Once he was sheltered from the elements by its sprawling branches and leaves, he looked for the source again.

He could see a woman wearing a jacket and carrying an umbrella heading his way. Quincy's vision wasn't the best, and the inclement weather wasn't helping his sight.

As the woman got closer, Quincy realized who it was.

"Lawana, is that you?"

"Yeah, it's me," Lawana replied. "I've been out here for an hour looking for you."

"How'd you know I was here?"

"C'mon, Quincy. Don't play dumb. You know who told me where to find you."

Quincy didn't reply. He and Lawana's relationship had always been contentious. One would stand a better chance of seeing a King Cobra and Mongoose hanging out together before witnessing Lawana and Quincy act civil towards each other.

Lawana tried to maintain her balance as she walked across the soggy grass. Dressed in skin tight jeans, a form fitting top, and four inch stilettos, she looked like a fish out of water. With each step she took, her heels seemed to sink deeper into the soil.

"I see you haven't changed," said Quincy as he shook his head and tried not to laugh at Lawana as she struggled to stay vertical. He extended his hand and allowed her to grab hold for leverage. "You are the only person I know who would come to a park wearing high-heel pumps."

"Yeah, well I guess some things never change," Lawana replied.

Quincy walked over to his shopping cart and removed a newspaper. He then walked over to his bench, took sheets and wiped the puddles off. The remaining pieces of newspaper were spread across the bench to serve as a barrier between the damp seat and Lawana's pants.

"Have a seat," said Quincy.

"Thanks," said Lawana as she sat. "Wow, you are more chivalrous now than you were back in the day."

"Let's cut to the chase, Lawana. Why are you here?"

Lawana wasn't enthused about being in that park so she didn't protest Quincy's insistence on skipping the small talk.

"Look, I know you spoke to QJ, and told him about everything that went on in the past between you and Carmen. Now, I'm not going to sit here and pretend that I agree with you telling that child about *grown folk* issues, but I do feel it's a good thing that he at least knows you are alive."

"Oh really? Considering the fact that you are the main person who helped Carmen bury me in the first place, I find it hard to believe that all of a sudden you are cool with my resurrection."

"Yes, I am the one who encouraged Carmen to tell that lie, and I helped her keep up the lie for all these years. I'm not proud of my role, but I still stand by my decision. When you never returned, it looked like a good decision. You do recall that you never returned, don't you?"

"Look Lawana, did you come here to rub my face in my mistakes? Well, I'm gonna steal your thunder. Yes, I was wrong for abandoning my son. It doesn't matter what Carmen did to me, I should have dug deeper, and found a way to set aside my feelings towards her and focused on being a good father to QJ."

Lawana didn't reply. Back when he was married to Carmen, Lawana always found his confidence and know-it-all attitude to be overbearing. She eagerly urged Carmen to flirt and mingle with other men back when they were all in their 20's. But that was then. She has changed and much to her surprise, she could tell that Quincy had changed. Was it humility born from poverty or wisdom? She wasn't sure, but she liked his new air.

"So, what can you tell me about Cookie? Has she changed much? Does she still go by that nickname?"

"She answers to it, but I don't think she hears it often because only a few of her closest friends knew about it. I doubt if most of the people she met after you left have heard it.

"And to answer your question, yes, she has changed; especially since she hooked up with Terry. She just isn't the same person. She doesn't act the same. She doesn't like to do the same stuff we used to."

"Yeah, I heard about Terry. QJ was tellin' me about him."

"What else has QJ told you about Terry?"

"Not much. I know they don't get along."

"That's an understatement. Trying to get them to be civil towards each other is harder than getting a White supremist to raise a black child."

"It's that bad?"

"Worse. I don't like my godson around all that hostility."

"I don't like it either," said Quincy, as the feeling of guilt rushed over him like a huge wave.

"Is that all he's told you?"

"Yeah. What else is there to know?"

"Several things. Did QJ tell you that he and Terry have had fights?"

"No. Verbal or physical?"

"Both."

Quincy's shoulders became tense. The Zulu warrior in him was starting to appear right there on that bench.

"That ma'fucka has been hitting my son?"

"They had a bad fight yesterday. QJ is living with me now. The fight was pretty bad," said Lawana, as she watched Quincy's leg begin to fidget. The exact reaction she was hoping to get from him. "Like I said, that boy needs you… so does his mama."

Quincy was too angry to reply. Lawana knew she'd struck an emotional chord so she continued her assault.

"You know it's never too late," said Lawana as she looked at the busy streets.

"Too late for what?"

"It's never too late for you to come back."

Quincy shook his head in agreement. "For a long time I thought it was too late, but lately I've had a change of heart."

"What caused you to change your way of thinking?" asked Lawana.

"Some cats I've met recently. One of the brothas was out here on the streets with me. He got in my ear and made me think. But he's dead now. The other brothas that convinced me I can still be there for QJ are..."

"Are what?"

"...in the church."

"In the church? You've been going to church?"

The look on Lawana's face and her tone caused Quincy to chuckle. His laugh made her giggle.

"Somethin' like that."

"Wow."

"You ain't gotta say it like that. You make it sound like I'm the devil's son."

"I'm not sayin' that, but I don't remember you being into church."

"Well, I wouldn't qualify as some type of bible toting brotha, but I've been attending these men's group meetings over at Ebenezer Baptist."

"Ebenezer Baptist?"

"Yeah. It's over there on..."

"I know where it is. I know some people who attend," Lawana replied, with a pensive look on her face.

"Are you alright? You look constipated."

"Nawh, nawh, my mind just drifted for a second."

"Anyway, I met a brotha named Terrance who goes to Ebenezer. He runs a men's group called H.A.B.U. I've been going to the meetings and learning more about how to conquer my demons and how to be a better father."

Lawana appeared to have drifted into another trance. Quincy started snapping his fingers to bring her back.

"Earth to Lawana. Are you still with me?"

"Oh, yeah. I'm listening. Umm, speaking of your *demons*, how are you dealing with your addiction?"

"It's been hard. I quit the drugs a few years ago, but I'm still battling the alcoholism. I haven't had a drink in a week."

"That's good. My dad could never kick his alcoholism. I don't think he ever stopped drinking for more than 48 hours. I applaud you for fighting it for a week."

"Thanks."

"Look, Quincy. I want to apologize for my role in driving a wedge between you and Carmen when we were all younger. I was a bad influence on her back then. I can admit that now. I'm sorry."

"So, is that why you came here today? To apologize for drama that happened ten years ago."

"I came here to do a couple of things; apologize to you was the first thing. I also wanted to encourage you to stay connected to your son. That boy needs you. He really does. I can see the tug of war that's going on. He's got Carmen on one end and those little thugs he hang with on the other."

"Yeah, I met his thug friends."

"I heard. Those little boys are destined for the penitentiary. If QJ doesn't get his act together he's going to be their cell mate. He needs a positive male role model. They both need you."

"I know that my son needs me. He's my primary motivation for turning my life around. As far as Carmen is concerned, that's the past."

"It doesn't have to be."

"What? You're trippin'."

"Do you still love her?"

Lawana's admission that QJ had been beaten by Terry and her query about his feelings regarding Carmen made

Quincy nervous. He pulled out a cigarette to help calm his nerves.

"Lawana, why are you fuckin' with me? You know I've always loved Carmen. She was my first and only love. I would have given my life for that woman and you know it. I never stopped loving her."

Lawana looked over at Quincy and noticed tears starting to well up in his eyes. This wasn't the same man she once despised. This man had changed.

"It's not too late to get her back. I know for a fact that Carmen held out hope that you would return to her for years. She rarely dated. She missed you. Now, I'll admit that when she did come out of her shell, she was eager to explore dating different people. But, I've always felt they were only replacements for you. She needed someone to occupy her heart."

"Isn't she engaged?"

"If that's what you wanna call it. Terry doesn't deserve Carmen. You can still get her back."

"Yeah right."

"I'm serious, Quincy. The question is do you want her back? Better yet, do you want to reunite the family you walked away from?"

"Yes," Quincy replied as he finally quit fighting and allowed a tear to run free.

"Do you want my help?" Lawana asked.

With the cigarette dangling on his bottom lip and bouncing every time he spoke, Quincy wiped his tears and replied, "Will you help me?"

Lawana opened her purse and wrote down her address on a sheet of paper. "Here is my address. I live in a three bedroom house on Dumaine Street. QJ is staying in one of my guest rooms. I still have one free. It's yours if you want it."

Lawana gave Quincy the paper, and then stood. The rain that had been pelting the pavement stopped—leaving only the soggy ground for her to manipulate on the way back to her car. Quincy remained seated and stared at the paper. He was both shocked and scared.

"I'm serious, Quincy. QJ needs you and although she doesn't know it, so does Carmen. I helped break the two of you up; the least I can do is try to bring y'all back together.

"Here is $50. It's all I have on me now. Use it to get you somethin' to eat and get yourself together. I want you come to my house the day after tomorrow. I will have everything set up for you. You can stay with me for a few weeks. That will give you some time to reconnect with QJ, and get yourself together so you can go and get your woman."

Lawana turned and walked away. Quincy sat on that bench holding a $50 bill in one hand, and Lawana's address in the other. His mouth held his diminishing cigarette while his eyes held tear drops just begging to get out. His heart held bottled up feelings for Carmen, and his mind held memories of the times he and his family once shared and life without his wife and son.

Quincy's life was changing for the better just as quickly as it had taken a turn for the worse. But, as with any change, the path can be bumpy. Quincy would have to maintain focus while fighting off his demons as he made the long, arduous trek that awaited him. Even he questioned whether or not he could.

Chapter 14

Quincy arrived at Lawana's shortly before nightfall—minus the shopping cart. He used the $50 she'd given him to purchase underwear, a few t-shirts, socks, toiletries, and a duffel bag to put it all in. He was as nervous as a young boy arriving at his date's home on prom night.

The scent of fried chicken was seeping through the door frame. It was Quincy's favorite. Once he got his paws into a piece of dark meat, he didn't let up until the marrow had been sucked out of the bone. His stomach started growling the moment he envisioned himself biting into a thick juicy leg.

"Hey, Quincy," said Lawana with a huge welcoming grin. "Come on in. I got your bedroom ready. You are just in time for dinner. I fixed fried chicken, red beans and rice, and corn bread. I'm tellin' you now; I am not the best cook so you can save all of your sarcastic remarks."

Quincy walked in and marveled at the décor of Lawana's home. He didn't know what Lawana did for a living, but whatever she was doing definitely accommodated her expensive taste.

"Wuz up?" said QJ as he walked into the living room. "Lawana told me she saw you at the park, and that you were coming. But, I didn't think you would show up."

"Well, I'm here… son," Quincy replied, and then extended his hand.

QJ frowned and looked at Quincy's hand like he saw manure smeared on it.

"So, you're gonna leave me hangin'?" asked Quincy.

QJ stood silently for a few seconds longer. The mood was awkward, but to Quincy's credit, he didn't let the boy off the hook. He kept his hand extended.

Recognizing his father was determined to get a hand shake, QJ went over and slightly grasped Quincy's fingers and then released. He shook Quincy's hand the way an infant grabs an adult's fingers.

"Is that how you shake a man's hand?"

"What?"

"Is that how you shake a man's hand? That was pretty weak to me. A little girl has a stronger grip than that."

QJ was surprised by the question. Quincy's hand was still extended. QJ glanced at his father's extended hand, and then looked into Quincy's eyes.

"Man you trippin'," he said, and then turned to walk away.

Quincy immediately thought about the H.A.B.U. meeting and the things Brotha Nelson said. It was happening. The resistance Brotha Nelson spoke of was transpiring right before Quincy's eyes. Brotha Nelson's words were getting louder in Quincy's ear.

If you think you're going to regain his trust by being nice and allowing him to disrespect you — either overtly or in subtle ways — you're sadly mistaken.

The only way you will regain your son's trust and respect is by re-establishing your lead role.

"QJ," Quincy exclaimed in a deep aggressive tone. "I asked you if that was the way you shake a man's hand."

QJ stopped in his tracks and turned around. It was clear the boy didn't know whether to get defensive or acquiesce to Quincy's stance. The two of them stood about six feet apart staring at each other like two gun fighters in an old western movie; each waiting for the other to blink.

Lawana stood in the hallway watching the scene as she held her breath. *C'mon, QJ, shake his hand, baby.*

QJ looked back at Lawana. He was hoping she'd bail him out, but to her credit, she didn't intervene. She hated QJ's lack of respect for his elders. She watched her godson become more disrespectful with each passing year. Carmen was a terrible disciplinarian, and often relied on Lawana to be the heavy hand with QJ. A role she reluctantly assumed over the years because it was clear to her that someone had to strike fear in the child.

Lawana was hoping QJ and Quincy would have a moment like this, but even she was surprised that it would happen before Quincy had a chance to put down his bag.

QJ glanced at her again. "Man, this dude's trippin'," he said, expecting Lawana to co-sign his sentiment.

Lawana looked back at him with a blank stare. She let him know that he was on his own.

Quincy's look was steely; he was going to stand there with hand extended until his son greeted him properly.

QJ was clearly surprised and nervous. He waited a few more seconds and then slowly walked towards his father. He clutched Quincy's hand. The two of them locked gazes— Alpha Male versus Alpha Male.

"Lord, have mercy," Lawana mumbled. "This is too much testosterone for me."

While Lawana retreated to the kitchen to prepare their dinner plates, Quincy and QJ stood in the living room sizing each other up. They just stood there gripping each other's hand.

"That's better," Quincy said as he finally shook his son's hand.

QJ rolled his eyes and finally released. The first show down was over—point to Quincy. But, this was just the battle; the war was far from over.

Quincy went into the guest bedroom assigned to him. He was always a neat freak, so his clothes were folded and placed into the drawers like he was a soldier at boot camp.

Lawana stuck her head into the bedroom. "Dinner is ready. You can use the bathroom at the end of the hallway to wash up."

"Thanks."

"By the way, I took the liberty of buying you a couple shirts and a few pairs of jeans — you look like you are about a 36" waist. Hopefully they fit. I hung them up in the closet. There are also some shirts hanging up that my ex-boyfriend left. He's been out of my life for a year. He didn't come back and get them so as far as I'm concerned he doesn't want them. You can have whatever you can fit."

"Well, I'm gonna take a shower if that's okay with you."

"No problem. Like I said, the bathroom is right down the hall. There are towels in the cabinet. Everything you need should be easy to find. We will wait until you're finished before we start eating."

"Thanks, Lawana. I appreciate this."

"No problem. Thanks for coming," Lawana replied and winked.

Quincy went into the bathroom and sat on the closed toilet lid for a few minutes. He looked at the bathroom like he'd never seen one before. He rubbed his hand across the counter top. After retrieving a wash towel from the cabinet he buried his face in it. A springtime scent infiltrated his nostrils.

It had been years since he'd taken a hot shower. He stood motionless as the water shot from the shower head and splashed on his chest and face. The steam filled the bathroom and made the mirror frosty white.

Quincy placed both hands on the wall as he allowed the water to douse his dirty hair. He poured a glob of shampoo into the palm of his rough hands, and then lodged his foam covered fingers into his nappy hair. His fingers massaged his dirty scalp. It felt so good he let out a low-pitched moan.

The water beneath his feet turned into brown puddles as the dirt that had accumulated from years of sleeping under bridges and on park benches broke away from his skin and hair, and escaped down the drain.

Quincy emerged from the bathroom feeling as fresh and clean as a newborn baby. His pores rejoiced. His hair had been denied shampoo for so long it begged for more. The filth that had been camping out under his fingernails was gone. He still needed a good manicure, but that could wait. Quincy was just happy to be able to walk around without smelling his own funk.

Quincy walked into the dining room to see QJ and Lawana sitting there with plates of food waiting for him.

"Wow, you're finished. I was starting to wonder if you'd drowned in the shower," said Lawana, and laughed.

"Yeah, I needed that."

"You ain't lying," said QJ sarcastically.

Quincy ignored his son's flippant comment and sat down. The meal looked awesome. Lawana went all out to prepare a meal fit for a king.

"Let's pray," Lawana said.

"Take off your hat, son."

QJ looked at Quincy like he'd asked him to pick up a snake.

"What?"

"I said, *remove your hat.*"

"Whatever!" QJ replied.

"Boy, take that damn hat off your head!" Lawana barked, and then snatched the hat off. "Now bow your head so I can say grace."

QJ glared at Quincy like he wanted to jump across the table and strike him. He rolled his eyes and then closed them, bowing his head at the same time.

"Lord, we thank You for this food You've allowed us to receive. I also wanna say thank You Father for bringing the three of us here together this evening. We pray, Father that the sharing of this meal will symbolize the first step in the healing process for us all. In Jesus' name we pray, Amen."

"Amen," Quincy said.

QJ said nothing. He reached for the hot sauce and ketchup and poured them both over his red beans and rice.

"That's gross," said Lawana.

"This is how I like it," QJ replied. "You don't know what you missin'."

Quincy chewed his food slow. Unsure how many more hot meals he'd receive, he tried to savor it. Lawana tried to make small talk to break the ice, but the tension that filled the air reigned supreme.

Halfway through dinner, QJ did something that would make the scene take a turn for the worse. He belched. It was one of those extended smelly belches. When he finally finished he laughed as if it was the funniest thing he'd ever done.

"That's nasty, QJ!" Lawana shouted. "Say, *excuse me!*"

QJ was laughing too hard to say anything. Slapping the table. Clutching his stomach. Behaving like he was watching Eddie Murphy in concert.

"QJ, *say excuse me*," said Quincy as he stared at his disrespectful offspring.

"What?" QJ asked.

"That was rude. I know your mama taught you better than that."

"How would you know *what* my mama taught me? You weren't around."

"QJ, stop it!" said Lawana in an attempt to defuse the situation before it got out of control.

"I'm gonna say it, but not because this deadbeat nigga told me to."

"What?" Quincy asked.

"You heard me!" QJ retorted. "Dog, you don't run nothin' here. You ain't been around in years."

"QJ, stop it!" Lawana said again, almost pleading.

"Nawh, Lawana, this dude is trippin'! You've been gone for a decade, and now you wanna come around tryin' to regulate. You ain't nothin' but a damn bum. You ain't shit to me!"

Lawana had heard enough. She slapped Quincy in the face. It was the only way she knew to make him shut up. The smack echoed throughout the house.

QJ's anger took over. He sat there stunned for a few seconds and then took his hand and knocked his plate and drink off the table. He looked like a child running down a grocery store aisle swiping canned goods of the shelf.

Angry and embarrassed, QJ stood up and walked away from the table. He made a beeline for his bedroom. He slammed the door behind him.

Quincy was incensed by his son's behavior. The boy was totally out of control and needed to be dealt with. He pushed his chair away from the table and attempted to stand up. QJ was about to get jacked up and Lawana knew it.

"No, Quincy," said Lawana, and grabbed Quincy's hand. "Let him go. Just leave him alone for now."

Quincy reluctantly sat back down. His appetite was gone. He had a Prince that needed to be reminded that it was awhile before he'd become the King.

"Lawana, I'm sorry about that. The boy is out of control."

"Quincy, just give him some time to calm down. This is new for him."

"It's new for me too, but that doesn't give him an excuse to disrespect either one of us."

"His actions weren't directed at me, they were meant to offend you. I just got caught in the crossfire. The boy has struggled to deal with the fact that his father—whom he thought was dead—is alive. He's also struggling to understand why you didn't make your presence known for years. I know this is a tough pill to swallow, but it is what it is.

"For the record, I agree that QJ is in need of discipline. Hell, he could probably use a few weeks at somebody's boot camp. But, you are not going to change him overnight. This transition is going to take time."

"I hear you, Lawana. But at the rate that boy is going, I may not have that much time."

"QJ's a good kid, he just needs some guidance. That's why God brought you back into his life. It's gonna work out."

"I hope you're right."

"I know I'm right," Lawana replied, and then stood up. "Now, I'm going to put these dishes away and clean up my kitchen. While I'm doing that you can start cleaning up this mess your child made."

Chapter 15

Five days had elapsed since the Civil War had broken out in Carmen's home, and although she was happy QJ left the house that evening, her heart was now aching more than her face did from the blow she'd received.

Carmen heard QJ say he was headed to Lawana's house, but she needed confirmation. She wanted to knock on the door or call Lawana to make sure QJ was okay, but she and Lawana still weren't on speaking terms.

Like a thief casing out a bank, Carmen parked down the street from Lawana's house. She just needed to see her child. If QJ didn't walk out that front door by eight o'clock that morning, Carmen was prepared to break down Lawana's front door if she needed to.

The clock on the dashboard of her car seemed stuck on 7:46 A.M. As the time slowly crept closer and closer to eight o'clock, her heart rate increased. What if he wasn't at Lawana's house? What if he'd run away? What if he was now living on the streets like his father? Each *what if* thought, caused Carmen to grip her steering wheel even tighter.

When Lawana's front door opened, and QJ walked out wearing his customary baggy jeans, oversized shirt, and baseball cap, Carmen closed her eyes and rested her forehead on her steering wheel. Her child was accounted for and safe. She could rest easily now that she knew he was living under the watchful eye of Lawana. She drove away breathing easier.

Later on that evening, her anxiety returned. She missed QJ. She'd seen him from afar, but she needed to feel him.

Carmen looked at the telephone on her nightstand. After their argument, she hadn't thought about dialing Lawana's phone number. But, things had changed. Her only child was now living with her former best friend. Well, using the word *former* may have been somewhat of a stretch, but their friendship was definitely on life support.

I need to talk to my child. I miss him so much. I need to hear his voice — let him know I still love him. Lawana's still mad at me and may not answer the phone when she sees my number on the caller I.D.

I'll just ask her how he's doing. I know Lawana won't let him run her house or act disrespectfully, but he's still my responsibility and I need to let her know that he chose to come over there — I didn't need her assistance.

After mulling over the situation in her mind a few minutes longer, Carmen finally broke down and called Lawana's home.

"Hello."

"Umm, hello Lawana. This is Carmen. I'm just calling to check on QJ, I know he's been there since the fight between him and Terry."

"Yeah, he's doing fine. You know I'm gonna take care of him."

"Yeah, I know."

There was an awkward silence born from the tension between the two ladies.

"Ummm, look Lawana, about our argument the other day. I want to…"

"Forget about it. The conversation got ugly, and it didn't need to be that way. You are a grown woman, and you can handle your relationship the way you see fit. I was alerting you to something I saw. What you do with the information is up to you. I've moved past that phone call.

"Right now, my concern lies with QJ. He is very upset and confused right now. I'm just trying to be a safe haven for him."

"I know and I appreciate that. However, I do want him to come home. He's been there for nearly a week. What are your thoughts about when he will be ready to come back?"

"Honestly Carmen, I don't know. He's welcome to stay longer, but you are his mother and if you want him to come home, you have every right to come and get him. That's a decision you are going to have to make — I'm not touching it.

"I will say this, the boy hates Terry. I can foresee him resisting if he thinks Terry is going to be there when he returns. He thinks you chose Terry over him."

"That's not true."

"I know it's not true. I know how much you love QJ, but he believes it's true. The more I think about it, it's probably best if he stays another week. That will give me time to work on his attitude."

"Yeah, you're probably right."

"Well, it's settled. I will bring QJ home next Sunday. In the meantime, try to rest your nerves."

"Okay. Lawana. I…"

"Yeah, I love you too. Now go get some rest and stop worrying about him. I got this."

Carmen disconnected the call feeling relieved that QJ was doing okay. She was also happy that Lawana seemed as eager to end their feud as she was.

Lawana hung up the phone feeling better about the situation too. She'd given Carmen the update she needed, and the two of them had figuratively kissed and made up. The focus was back where it should have been — on QJ.

There was one update Lawana conveniently forgot to give Carmen. She avoided mentioning that QJ wasn't her only house guest. Lawana knew that if she'd told Carmen that Quincy was living there with her and QJ, Carmen would have been banging on her front door before she could have completed her sentence. The peace treaty they'd just verbally signed would have been broken faster than the treaties between Israel and Palestine.

Lawana had a plan. A plan that she felt would change QJ's, Quincy's, and Carmen's lives, for the better. Lawana intended to give QJ and Quincy enough time to form a bond. She was then going to coach Quincy on how to win back Carmen. An ambitious plan? Yes, but one she thought she could pull off. She may have told Carmen that she could handle her personal life in the way she deemed necessary, but she didn't really mean it.

Lawana despised Terry. As long as she had a heart beat, she was going to work to get Carmen out of that relationship—even if it meant she had to help her former arch rival, Quincy, get back on his feet.

A full day had passed since QJ and Quincy's blow up at the dining room table. The two avoided each other like the plague. Sleeping in adjacent bedrooms allowed them to gauge when the coast was clear to walk down the hallway and into the kitchen; when to go to the bathroom without bumping into each other; and avoid any unexpected encounters.

QJ sat on a chair in his bedroom, headphones blasting rap music in his ears as he stared out the window. This pensive state was rather unusual for this normally carefree child. Over the years he'd perfected the art of not caring enough about any of life's challenges. Making failing grades in school didn't bother him. Being at odds with his devoted mother didn't bother him. But the re-emergence of Quincy in his life was definitely taking an emotional toll on the boy.

Quincy stood outside of QJ's bedroom door peeking at his son. Knowing he was the reason the boy was in such poor spirits made Quincy's heart ache.

As he stood there watching his child like a stalker, Lawana gently touched his shoulder.

"I know this is tough," she whispered. "But he needs you. He needs you more than he realizes. You've got to be the bigger person, Quincy."

"I know," Quincy whispered.

"Well if you know why are you standing out here instead of in there?"

Quincy nodded in agreement, and then took a deep breath. He slowly entered QJ's bedroom. QJ's book bag was partially opened on the bed. Graded school papers were sprawled across the bed. Quincy could see huge grades scribbled in red ink at the top of each paper. An English exam had a "D" written on the top of the paper. A Math exam had an "F" on the top of the paper.

Quincy picked up the math exam and started examining the paper. There were ten algebra questions. QJ got the first question correct, but it was clear to Quincy, a former math whiz, that QJ simply got discouraged and gave up on the next question. He didn't even try to finish the exam.

"What are you doing?" QJ asked, startling his father.

"Oh, nothing," Quincy nervously replied. "I was just coming in to say hello. I noticed your school work on the bed."

QJ stood up and snatched the exam out of Quincy's hand. He then shoved the exam and all of the exposed paperwork back into his book bag.

"You don't have to worry about this," said QJ.

"Well son, it looks like you are having trouble in math. I can help you if you need it."

"Yeah, right," QJ replied, and shook his head. "You can't help yourself. How are you gonna help me? It doesn't matter anyway — I'll just go to summer school."

Quincy was so ashamed at his role in the boy's poor attitude he ignored the disrespect being displayed. He needed to break down this wall somehow.

At that very moment, Quincy started thinking about his old friend Scoop. But this time it wasn't any of Scoop's words that came to mind, it was what he and Scoop used to do together — play chess. Unlike checkers, in chess, most games were won by taking an indirect approach to capture the opponents King. Charging head first was a sure way to have your pieces taken, which would allow an opponent to have an easy victory.

In his efforts to break down QJ's walls, Quincy had been charging head first. He was playing checkers when he should have been playing chess. It was at that moment he decided to change his strategy. He was going to earn his son's respect and confidence without looking like he was trying.

"Yeah, summer school is an option — if you wanna spend your summer sitting in a classroom when you could be hanging with your friends and kickin' it with that cute girlfriend of yours," said Quincy as he turned to walk out of the room. "How much does summer school costs these days?"

"I don't know," QJ replied, with a look of disinterest in both Quincy and what he was saying.

"I'm sure it's somewhere in the ballpark of $150 to $200. I would think you'd rather have your mom hook you up with some of those Play Station games."

QJ looked at his father. Quincy's comment got his attention. Quincy saw his son's curiosity kick in.

"If that's the type of math that's gonna land you in summer school, then that's a waste to me — especially when the only thing you're missing is one simple formula."

"When was the last time you did any kind of math?" QJ asked, his comments were meant to be sarcastic, but they revealed his desire for help.

Quincy smirked. "Yeah, it has been awhile. Do you know what I did for a living back when I was working?"

QJ didn't answer—continuing to pretend to act disinterested.

Quincy stopped at the door with his hand on the knob. He didn't really want to leave, and if QJ had turned around he would have seen his father's fake attempt to leave. Quincy's acting was poor. If it had been a movie set the director would have yelled *cut* a dozen times.

"Well, I don't know if your mom told you, but I used to be an Accountant. Math was my thing in high school. That's why I know you are just one formula away from going from an F to an A."

"What?"

Quincy inched a few feet away from the door. "Yeah, I saw that you did the first question right. It looked like you were halfway through the second problem and then you just stopped."

"That teacher is stupid!" QJ blurted out. "She doesn't know what she's doing. She doesn't explain the stuff right."

QJ's comments were typical of a high school student who was too embarrassed to admit he didn't comprehend the material. Rather than ask for assistance, he chose to paint the teacher as incompetent. Quincy saw this opening and pounced on it.

"Yeah, I had teachers like that when I was in high school. I was a junior when I ran across one teacher that taught me one simple formula that made it all make sense. Hell, I was pissed off when I finally saw how easy it was— my damn teachers made the shit harder than it had to be.

"Can I see that exam again?" asked Quincy, and stuck out his hand.

QJ looked at Quincy's hand and then at his bag. The boy was as stubborn as a mule. He wanted to acquiesce without looking like it. Time stood still as QJ contemplated giving in. The scene was similar to their encounter in the living room when Quincy stuck his hand out to shake QJ's.

QJ thought about spending time in summer school. He wanted to hang out with Tia—maybe even get a few more shots at seeing her panties. Being stuck in summer school would definitely derail that plan.

Although QJ's decision to allow Quincy to help him was tainted with misguided pubescent thoughts, he figured it beat allowing Algebra to wreck his summer.

Quincy was aware that the thoughts of being in summer prison were his son's primary motivation for letting down his guard, but he didn't care. *By any means necessary* was his motto. He'd found a way inside of QJ's fortress, now it was time to make his presence known.

QJ opened his book bag and pulled out the exam. He gave the exam to Quincy and reclined in his chair.

"Awwh, yeah. I remember this stuff. You're supposed to multiply polynomials right."

"Yeah."

"Let me guess, your teacher taught y'all to multiply the outside number with the inside number and all of that other confusing crap."

"Yeah, she was sayin' something like that. A lot of people didn't understand what she was saying. She doesn't like to admit that she doesn't know what she's doing so she just keeps teaching this stuff her own way even though she knows we don't understand it."

The more QJ talked, the more Quincy reeled him in. Like a chess player who knows that *checkmate* is only a few moves away, Quincy kept a serious look on his face when deep down he wanted to jump for joy.

"I feel you. Most of the teachers can't teach a lick. Man, I can teach you how to do this in five minutes. All you need to learn is the F.O.I.L. formula."

"What?"

"F.O.I.L. Like aluminum foil. Most people are visual learners. Most math teachers are so into crunching numbers that they ignore the fact that people learn best when you can associate what you're learning with everyday stuff.

"Whenever you see this type of math problem just think about aluminum foil."

"That's stupid," said QJ.

"I thought it was stupid too, until I tried it and got A's on every polynomial test I took afterwards. Give me a pencil, and I'll show you what I'm talkin' about."

QJ gave Quincy a pencil to write with. Quincy gestured for QJ to come sit next to him on the end of the bed — a risky move, but he didn't have anything to lose at that point. It was all or nothing and Quincy decided to go for it.

When QJ came over, Quincy knew he was one move away from *checkmate*. QJ sitting next to him was the equivalent of *check*.

"F.O.I.L. stands for: first, outer, inner, and last. Let's use the second problem you had trouble with," said Quincy, and then went to work.

Quincy mulled over the problem a little longer, pretending he was deep in thought. Truth of the matter, he could do the problem in his sleep.

Once he determined he'd displayed a level of concern that would convince the boy that he was serious, he helped QJ work on the following problem:

$(3z + 5) \times (2z + 7)$

1.   *First* = $3z \times 2z = 6z^2$
2.   *Outer* = $3z \times 7 = 21z$
3.   *Inner* = $5 \times 2z = 10z$
4.   *Last* = $5 \times 7 = 35$

$6z^2 + 21z + 10z + 35 =$

$6z^2 + 31z + 35$

Any concerned parent can relate to the agony felt when his or her child doesn't understand school work, and no matter how hard you try to explain it, the child doesn't get it. Conversely, there are few things on God's earth that can make a parent feel better than witnessing them go from a state of frustration and confusion to enlightenment.

QJ fought as hard as he could to fight back the smile his usually flippant mouth was forming. But pure joy can't be bridled. He'd been struggling with Algebra since the first week of school, and this was the first time he actually understood any of it. Sure, this was just one type of Algebra problem. But his sudden ability to understand it gave him hope. Like a man trapped in a cave that has spent weeks trying to dig out; when the urge to quit is upon him, even the slightest glimmer of light can provide enough motivation to keep digging.

Quincy spent the next hour going over each problem with his son. By the seventh problem, QJ had mastered the F.O.I.L. concept. Quincy was convinced that if QJ was given the opportunity to retake the exam, he'd pass with flying colors.

During his college days, Quincy tutored a lot of athletes in math. The experience afforded him a chance to work side by side with several instructors. What Quincy learned during that time was most teachers root for their students. Sure there were some that got a perverse pleasure out of failing students. But the overwhelming majority of teachers wanted their students to succeed. Armed with that knowledge, Quincy proposed something to his son.

"Man, I wish I would have known this before the test," said QJ as he studied the paper.

"It's not too late," Quincy replied.

"What do you mean? You think that teacher is gonna let me take the test again? You trippin. Ms. Lindsay is the meanest teacher at that school. She ain't gonna let me take it over."

"Have you been failing her class all year?"

"Yep. I've failed every exam. She doesn't like me."

"Why do you say that?"

"Because she doesn't. Every day in class she singles me out. She will ask a question to the entire class, and then ignore everyone who has their hands up ready to answer it—just so she can embarrass me.

"One day I wasn't feelin' good, and I had my head on the desk. This woman still called on me. She knew I wasn't feelin' good. She knew I hadn't been payin' attention. She just wanted to make me look bad."

"That's what you think?"

"That's what I know. I'm tellin' you, that woman just wants to fail me."

"Hmm... I know how to get her to allow you to take the exam over."

"How?"

"Before I start tellin' you my plan, I need to know if you would take it again."

QJ paused and contemplated his father's question. He wanted to take the exam, but the fear of failure had control of his mind. Quincy could see the trepidation on his child's face. Challenging math exams that are administered by challenging teachers can have that type of affect on a student. But, Quincy wasn't about to let his namesake give up.

Quincy yanked a sheet of paper out of one of the folders in QJ's bag. He walked over to the desk in the corner and got an ink pen. With his son looking on in bewilderment, Quincy wrote the following letter to this so called mean teacher that had QJ spooked:

Dear Ms. Lindsay,

My name is Quincy Washington Sr. I am Quincy's father. After years of being out of his life I am back now and trying to make up for lost time. One of the things he and I are tackling is his school work (attendance, study habits, etc.).

After looking at some of his graded exams tonight, I noticed that he is failing Algebra. Being a former Accounting major in college, I understand the importance of getting a strong math foundation. I know you've worked hard to help students like my son better understand this challenging topic. I also know that you can't do it alone — you need parental involvement. This is why I'm writing you.

Quincy and I have spent time studying. As a result, I think he had a breakthrough on the topic of multiplying Polynomials. I know he failed the exam you gave him last week, but I would really appreciate it if you would consider giving him a second shot at passing the test. I believe that if you selected ten new problems for him and gave him the necessary time to finish the exam after school, you will see improvement.

I've spoken to Quincy and explained to him that teachers have lives too, and you are not required to make this exception for him. However, if you could find some time to honor this request, I think you will see that it was worthwhile.

I appreciate the time you've spent thus far with my son, and I hope you will give this request some consideration. Thanks for all you do.

Respectfully submitted,
Quincy Washington Sr.

QJ read the letter and then looked at his father. Frowning as if he'd just bitten into an orange peel, the boy's anxiety became airborne.

"Are you serious?" QJ asked.

"Yep."

"Ms. Lindsay's gonna laugh at me if I give this to her," said QJ as he read the letter again. "And why are you tellin' her all of our business? You think she cares that you studied Accounting in college? She doesn't care about that."

"First of all, I don't think she's gonna laugh at the request. The odds are great that she never gets a letter like this from a parent. Hell, she may even be excited to get it.

"Secondly, I told her that I've been out of your life because it's the truth. If I had been there for you, you would already have this stuff figured out. So, that's my fault. I'm sure you haven't been the best student from a behavior perspective. That one sentence will shed some light on things for her and may even buy you a little needed sympathy.

"Last, but not least, telling her I was an Accounting major in college helps break down some stereotypes she may have already bought into. She needs to know that your father is educated, and majored in a math related subject. It gives her and me something in common even though we've never met. When people feel they can relate to you they are more inclined to work with you as opposed to against you. Son this is chess, not checkers."

"What does that mean?"

"It's a figure of speech. Checkers is reactive, chess requires strategy. It's going to take strategy to change this teacher's perspective of you. If you just do as I say this one time, and give the teacher this letter, you will see what I'm talkin' about."

QJ stared at the letter as he allowed his father's words to sink in. The boy was too naïve to realize that the strategy of rapport-building Quincy was attempting to use on his teacher was already being used on him.

"Alright," QJ finally replied. "I don't think it's going to work, but I'll give it to her."

Quincy decided to quit while he was ahead. He stood and exited the room without looking back.

QJ sat on the edge of the bed trying to figure how he'd gone from despising his father twenty four hours earlier, to having a lengthy discussion and doing math problems with him.

When Quincy walked into the living room he was greeted by a smiling Lawana. She grabbed a handful of popcorn out of her bowl, and rammed it in her mouth.

"Have a seat," she suggested.

Quincy sat down in a nearby recliner and smiled as he looked at the television. It wasn't the commercial that was showing that prompted the grin on his face; it was the realization that he'd actually made progress with his son.

"So how do you feel?"

"I feel good. I feel *real* good right now."

"I told you it could be done."

"Yes, you did."

"So are you ready for your next challenge?"

"What's that?"

Lawana took a sip of her drink to wash down the popcorn and then looked at Quincy. She knew her next question was about to throw him for a loop.

"Are you ready to win back your wife?"

"What?"

"You heard me. Are you ready to win back Carmen?"

"Hold up Lawana, one thing at a time. I just had a breakthrough with QJ and now you're already talkin' about me and Carmen getting back together. Don't you think I should try to get some type of job or something?"

Lawana was so anxious to get Terry out of Carmen's life that she inadvertently overlooked Quincy's employment status.

"Yeah, you do need a job. We can work on that. In the meantime, you need to be thinking about Carmen. Time is not on your side, bruh."

"No disrespect, but you were never a fan of she and I being together. Why have you changed your position?"

"True that," Lawana conceded. "I'll admit that I wasn't your biggest fan. But, I've changed and so has Carmen. Honestly, considering the time that has elapsed, I'm not sure if the two of you are right for each other. But, I know one thing, you are better for her than Terry."

"Really?" Quincy replied, staring at Lawana with a suspicious look on his face. His instincts told him Lawana wasn't just being nice to him because she'd changed. She must have had an ulterior motive.

"Why are you lookin' at me like that?"

"I'm just wonderin' what you have up your sleeve. Why don't you want Carmen and Terry to be together?"

"I just don't approve of the relationship. I don't think Terry is right for Carmen, and I know QJ feels the same way."

"You still haven't told me why you feel this way."

"Look, I just feel she can do better. And I can tell you now; QJ will never live under the same roof with Terry."

"Is Terry living with Carmen now?"

"Not yet. But, they spend a lot of time together."

"Aren't they getting married soon?"

Lawana waved her hand dismissively in Quincy's direction. "Married? Yeah right. That's what she is sayin', but I'm not even entertaining that. Carmen will probably hate me, but I'm going to do all I can to break that shit up. That's where you come in."

"Oh really?"

"Yep. I know for a fact that you were the love of that girl's life. At one time she worshipped the ground you walked on. On top of that, the two of you have a child together. When a woman has a baby with a man, that man will always maintain a place in that woman's heart.

"Now, the million dollar question is; do *you* want to win Carmen back?"

Quincy sat quietly as he pondered the question. Memories of happier times between him and Carmen flooded his mind. The day QJ was born. Their first family picnic. The concerts and movies the two of them attended. The intimate kisses and love making they shared. Memories a man never forgets when he truly loves a woman.

"Well? Do you want her back or not?"

"Yes," Quincy mumbled.

"I can't hear you," said Lawana antagonistically.

"I said, yes!" Quincy blurted out, a wide grin encompassing his face.

"That's what I'm talkin' bout. Say it like you mean it," replied Lawana with a chuckle. "Do you want me to help you get her back?"

"You think you can?"

"I can try. It ain't gonna be easy, but we won't know until we try. The first thing we have to do is get you back on your feet. You can't go at her lookin' destitute. You have to show her that you are your old self. We need her to get flashbacks of the way you used to be back when times were good between the two of you."

"I agree," said Quincy as he shook his head in agreement.

"As far as I'm concerned, you are halfway there Quincy. You are in a rehab program addressing your addictions. You got yourself cleaned up physically. I'm going to pay for you to get a haircut, manicure, and for you to get those crusty feet worked on this week. Combine that with the fresh clothes you have now, and I think you're set in that area.

"You aren't living on the streets anymore. I told you it was okay for you to stay here until you got your life together, and I meant that.

"You are already working on rebuilding your relationship with QJ. Believe me, that is a huge thing. That in itself puts you light years ahead of Terry. Once QJ becomes your advocate it's going to be hard for her to ignore you.

"The one thing that's missing is you having a job. We can work on that. I'm going to make some phone calls to a few friends of mine that work in Human Resources. I'm sure we can come up with something. You are one of the smartest brothas I know, so there is no doubt in my mind that you will eventually find work that suits your skills."

Quincy reclined back in the seat. His feet were elevated and his head was facing the ceiling. He closed his eyes as he processed everything Lawana was saying. He'd always wanted to reunite his family. He missed his wife and child. He missed being both a father and husband.

Without warning, Quincy's closed eyes filled with water and tears started to roll down his face. Lawana stopped chewing when she saw him cry. She could be as cold as ice when she wanted to be, but even she couldn't escape the emotions of the moment. Tears began to form in her scheming eyes and stream down her face.

Lawana's motives for facilitating Quincy's comeback had been questionable in the beginning, but now more than ever, she was committed to making this dream a reality. She reclined back in her chair and closed her eyes. Neither said a word. There was nothing left to be said.

Quincy was determined to pay back Lawana for her generosity. He didn't have the cash to compensate her for her generosity, but he had an innate desire to work. While standing outside smoking a cigarette, he started looking at Lawana's yard, fence, gutters, and shrubs. He'd figured out how to repay his debt.

That next morning Quincy was the first person out of bed. He searched high and low for Lawana's coffee maker. His search took him to a cabinet located in the far corner. Quincy finally found the coffee maker he wanted, but it also brought him in contact with something he wasn't expecting to see—a bottle of Cognac.

Quincy stared at the bottle as if he was staring at a bag of gold coins. His mouth became dry. Suddenly, he was thirsty for a sip. Just enough to wet his dry lips would satisfy his desire.

Lawana and QJ were still asleep so the chance of him getting caught was low. He examined the bottle to see if there were any marks on the bottle to gauge the liquor level. None in sight; Lawana wouldn't even notice.

A mental tug of war started to take place in his head.

I haven't had a drink in weeks. A little sip can't hurt. I can use a little sip right about now. No Quincy, you've been doing good. You've finally made some progress with your son. Why would you do something to mess that up? One little sip won't mess up your progress with QJ. But, what if they smell it on my breath? I should probably go and get the mouthwash and bring it in here so that I can wash my mouth out after I get a taste.

Quincy's desire to have a quick taste of the smooth liquor one the battle. He removed the coffee pot and Cognac from the cabinet and placed them both on the counter top. Quincy grabbed a coffee mug and sat it next to the liquor.

Go and get the mouthwash first, dummy.

Quincy turned around and took one step towards the hallway that lead to the bathroom and ran into Lawana.

"Hey, I didn't hear you," he said nervously.

Lawana was no dummy. She quickly realized what she'd walked in on. "Yeah, I know you didn't see me, but I see you."

Lawana walked over to the refrigerator and opened it up. She wasn't really looking for anything to eat or drink, her intent was to turn away long enough to allow Quincy to clean up the mess he was about to make.

"Umm, I was just about to make some coffee," Quincy replied, and then turned and put the Cognac back in the cabinet.

They engaged in small talk while the coffee brewed.

"Do you always get up this early?" Lawana asked.

"Yep. It's almost seven o'clock—you should be up already. I thought you said you had to get to work by eight o'clock."

"I said I'm *supposed* to be at work by eight. I didn't say that I actually *arrived* at eight."

Quincy laughed and slid Lawana's coffee cup over to her. "Well, this should wake you up."

Lawana took a sip and shouted, "Damn bruh! Are you sure this is coffee? This shit taste like mud."

"Coffee is supposed to wake you up," replied Quincy. "That's *real* coffee."

"Whatever. If this is real coffee, I'd rather drink grapefruit juice."

"Look, it's important to me that I pay you for allowing me to stay here. You know my money is kind of funny these days, but I wanna pay you. Here is a pen and some paper. I want you to write down at least three things you want me to do or fix around here. We can do this a few times a week until you run out of projects."

"You mean like a *To Do* list?" asked Lawana. "You don't have to tell me twice. You can cut and trim my grass. I have a lawnmower and edger in the garage that hasn't been touched in months. I usually let this little boy who lives up the street cut it, but he always leaves big ass gashes in my lawn.

"Ummm, let me see what else. Oh I know. You can fix that toilet in my bathroom—it keeps making that annoying noise—like it's always flushing. I have some tools in the garage. That's all I can think of now, but trust me, I'll have a list ready for you by the time I get home."

A few moments later, QJ came walking into the kitchen rubbing his eyes. Like all teenage boys, he was looking for the largest bowl he could find so he could fill it up with cereal.

"Good morning," Lawana said, reminding him that he needed to show some manners and address the adults in his presence.

"Good morning," QJ muttered.

"Good morning, son," said Quincy.

"Mornin'," QJ replied without looking at Quincy.

"Oh, hell no!" said Lawana. "That is a mixing bowl. You are not going to eat up all the cereal in two days. You'd better grab one of those smaller bowls and eat like normal people."

QJ did as he was told. He fixed a bowl of cereal and then walked back into his bedroom.

"You need to hurry up and eat so you can get ready for school. I'm going to drop you off on my way to work, and I'm leaving in about thirty minutes."

"That boy," said Quincy.

"I know. He doesn't like to follow rules, but he knows he doesn't have a choice as long as he's living here. Anyway, I'm going to get dressed so I can leave."

Lawana turned to walk out of the kitchen and then she stopped. "You know there is something else I need you to do."

"What's that? Just name it."

"Carmen has been raising QJ on her own all of these years, and at times it's been very hard. Don't get me wrong, she's a great mother, but I don't care how good at parenting a woman may be, there are just some things a woman cannot teach a young boy.

"I appreciate you doing chores around here, but I need you to commit to teaching your son a thing or two about being a young man. There are some basic things he has never learned. Things like the importance of opening doors for ladies; how to tie a necktie; and all of that male shit y'all men talk about."

Quincy chuckled, "I feel you. I'll make up my own list of things to address with him."

"Cool. And do me a favor—as long as you are black and breathing, don't you ever attempt to make me a cup of coffee again. You're tryin' to kill a sista in here."

"I hear you," Quincy said and laughed.

"Oh, one last thing," said Lawana.

"What?"

"Open that cabinet right there and pass me that bottle of Cognac. I wouldn't want you to get tempted and do something that you're gonna regret."

Quincy spent the entire day knocking out the things on Lawana's *To Do* list. Just as he was shoving the last pile of grass in a large garbage bag, he saw QJ approaching.

QJ was holding a sheet of paper in his hand. He was smiling and waving the paper.

"What's up?" Quincy asked. "You are usually walkin' around here lookin' like you mad at the world. Why you grinning?"

"That's why," he replied as he gave Quincy the paper.

It was an exam — an Algebra exam to be exact. Written at the top of the paper in bold red ink was an A. Next to the grade was a smiley face.

"That's what I'm talkin' 'bout!" shouted Quincy. "I told you that letter was gonna work. You gonna learn to respect my mind!"

QJ smiled and gave his father some dap. Quincy wasn't sure if he was happier about QJ's grade or the fact that he gave him dap. Rather than overanalyze the gesture, he just went with the flow.

"Yeah, I ain't gonna lie, I'm startin' to respect your mind," QJ replied.

"So how did it go down?"

"Well, it's my last class. So, I got there early and handed her the letter you wrote. At first she acted like she didn't wanna take it. I finally told her it was from my dad. She looked shocked that I even *had* a dad.

"The bell rung while she was reading and everyone else came in the class so I just sat down. She didn't say anything to me during the entire class. When the bell rung ending the class she told me to remain seated. All of my friends started laughing. They figured I was in trouble again.

"Anyway, she waited until everyone left and then she started writing problems on the board. She wrote five problems and told me every one was worth 20 points. She told me I had thirty minutes to do all of the problems. Whatever I scored would be my final grade."

"Wow. That means you could only afford to get one wrong. Were you nervous?"

"Hell yeah!" QJ blurted out. He responded like he was talking to one of his buddies. But at that very moment, a shift took place. Before Quincy could protest, QJ corrected himself. "Ooops, my bad. I mean, yeah I was nervous."

A warm feeling came over Quincy. The feeling wasn't from the harsh sun that was pounding his flesh. It was the internal warmth that's produced by one's spirit when God is showing up and showing out.

"I finished those problems in about 15 minutes. She was shocked. I cracked her face when I knocked out those problems she wrote on the board."

"That's one of the reasons I wrote that letter. I knew that if she saw with her own two eyes that you could do the test she would treat you differently."

"Oh, that reminds me," said QJ as he took off his book bag and pulled a letter from a side pocket. "She told me to give you this letter."

Quincy opened the letter and read it:

Dear Mr. Washington,

I don't know what you did, but the student that sat here and took this quiz in front of me today is not the same student that's been in my class all year.

I've always sensed Quincy had the ability to learn the work, but there always seemed to be something obstructing his desire. Your letter shed some light on that obstruction for me.

I appreciate the fact that you reached out to me. I will continue to work with Quincy and encourage you to do the same. Together, I know we can get him through this thing we "Math Nerds" call Algebra.

I will be praying for the two of you. Good luck.

Ms. Lindsay

Chapter 16

Quincy and QJ spent the next few days bonding. Within four days, Quincy had covered topics ranging from chivalry, to respect, to sex, to knot tying. He even started teaching the boy how to play what he called the greatest board game ever created—chess.

While Quincy and QJ sat in the bedroom playing a game of chess, Lawana sat on the phone with Carmen giving her an update on QJ.

"Yeah, girl. He's fine. I will drop him off at school in the morning. He knows that he's supposed to return to your house when he gets out.

"I've even been talking to him about accepting your relationship with Terry."

"Thanks," said Carmen in a glum tone. "I've been talkin' to Terry too. I plan to make both of them sit down when QJ comes back so that we can all talk. I need harmony in my house."

"I can't promise you he's going to be receptive, but I've been talkin' to him. His da…"

"What?"

Lawana nearly let the cat out of the bag. She still had not told Carmen that she'd been housing Quincy for the past few weeks. Unsure of how Carmen would react, she quickly tweaked her comment.

"Oh, I got distracted for a second. I was about to say that his damn head is so hard at times."

Mission accomplished. Carmen didn't suspect anything. She ignored Lawana's slip of the tongue like teenage drivers ignore stop signs.

"Girl, he is stubborn. He gets that from his father. Quincy was the same way," said Carmen.

Lawana's eyes widened. She'd been looking for an opportunity to gauge how receptive Carmen would be to discussing Quincy, and now she had the perfect segue.

"Speaking of Quincy, did you and QJ ever talk about him?"

"Unfortunately we didn't. I know that's something I'm gonna have to address with him when he returns."

"Yeah, I think you should. But, I got good news regarding that."

"What's that?"

"Well, since he's been here, QJ has been asking me a lot of questions about his father. I've been surprised at how curious he's been. He doesn't even seem angry anymore. He's just curious."

"What did he ask you?"

"Well, he asked me about Quincy's personality. I told him Quincy was often very serious. I also told him how smart his dad was. Girl, do you remember how smart Quincy was?"

"Yeah. He was one of the smartest people I've ever met," Carmen replied in a stuttered tone that indicated she was reflecting on the past as she spoke.

Lawana started pouring it on thick. She wanted to more than jog Carmen's memory; she wanted to shake it until her friend became choked up with emotion.

"I'm not trying to tell you how to handle your business, but I think you should definitely engage in a discussion about Quincy. I mean, the boy knows the truth now. On top of that, he's curious about his father. If you try to avoid the topic it may make him more rebellious. If you take the lead on the discussion it makes you look like you have nothing to hide."

Carmen sat there quietly. She didn't say a word. She was so quiet that Lawana thought she'd hung up.

"Hello. Are you still there?"

"Yeah, I'm here," Carmen replied. "I'm just listening to you."

"It's been awhile since we talked about Quincy. I'm just curious. Have you told Terry that Quincy is still alive?"

"No, I haven't. Honestly, I don't even know how to bring up the topic."

"Well, you're gonna have to bring it up soon."

"I know. I'll figure out something before QJ comes home."

"Umm Cee, can I ask you somethin' else?"

"Yeah. What?"

"Do you still think about Quincy? I mean, I know that a lot of time has passed, but girl you used to be crazy about that man. You used to get on my damn nerves talkin' about Quincy all day. I think that's part of the reason why I didn't like him."

Carmen started laughing. "I know. I had it bad back then."

"Shiiiit, you were a pain in the ass. But I can't deny— y'all made a beautiful baby together. No one can take that away. QJ is a handsome little boy. He's gonna be a heartbreaker."

"Giiirl, I know. These little girls be chasin' behind him right now."

"I know. He needs a man to talk to him about that transition from being a boy to a man. You can't talk to him, and you know Terry can't talk to him. It's too bad Quincy is in the condition he's in. That boy could use him."

"I know," Carmen replied, the sadness in her voice seeped through the phone line. "I'm just gonna have to figure out a way to get him the advice he needs."

"I'm just curious, what if Quincy got cleaned up?"

"What?"

"What if Quincy got cleaned up? I know y'all had all that drama, but you can't deny, QJ probably needs his father more than ever. If Quincy had his act together I'll bet he could get that boy straight."

"Yeah. You're probably right."

"I really believe that. Besides, QJ ain't the only person who needs to see Quincy," said Lawana, and then laughed.

"What?"

"You heard me. QJ ain't the only person that would like to see Quincy."

"Girl, please…"

"Whatever! You know if Quincy came back lookin' like he used to look you'd piss in your pants. I mean I'll admit, I couldn't stand his ass, but the brotha was handsome. Don't even try to sit here and pretend he wasn't."

Carmen laughed. "I'm not gonna say he wasn't. Quincy was very handsome. I remember the first time I saw him. That negro had me stuttering when he said hello."

"Girl I remember. Your ass was hooked from the first time you saw him. That's why I said what I said. If you knew Quincy was coming over you'd be in the mirror tryin' to fix your hair and pushing up your bra tryin' to get your cleavage to show."

"Whatever," said Carmen, releasing a light-hearted chuckle like a high school girl trying to deny her first crush. "If only life was that easy. It took me a long time to get over Quincy. I'm still angry over him leaving us the way he did."

"I can understand that, my friend. But, life is short. Everything happens for a reason. You gotta admit, the way all this went down seems like it came straight out of some novel or one of those made for television movies."

"You ain't lying."

"I didn't mean to stress you out with all of that talk about Quincy. It just came to my mind because QJ seems so eager to get to know him."

"It's okay," said Carmen. "It's complicated. I have so many unresolved feelings."

"I hear you," replied Lawana. She knew she'd accomplished her task. Carmen would go to bed with memories of Quincy bouncing around in her head. "I'm about to go. I got a lot to do at work tomorrow. I told QJ to go straight home after school. Let me know how it all works out."

"I will. Lawana…"

"Yeah, what's up?"

"Thank you. Thanks for being there for me and for QJ. I love you and I don't want to ever say or do anything to jeopardize our friendship again."

"I feel the same way. And I promise you, from now on, I'm gonna mind my business. My role is to support you and my godson. I love you too."

Lawana hung up the phone and headed towards QJ's bedroom. She could hear him and Quincy in the room talking and laughing. She smiled. She was happy to see their bond form. She even felt proud of her role.

"Umm, I hate to break up this little happy moment," said Lawana as she opened the bedroom door. "But QJ I need to talk to your father for a second."

"Fo sho," said QJ.

"I'm tired of whippin' on this youngster anyway," said Quincy as he stood. "I'm gonna crash after we talk."

"Whatever!" shouted QJ and laughed.

QJ stood and the two faced each other. After several tense moments over the past few weeks, their new-found friendship was finally consummated.

Quincy and QJ shook hands. It wasn't the traditional handshake. It wasn't the lukewarm handshake. It was the intimate handshake—the one that ended with their chins pressed into each other shoulders and their free hands affectionately tapping the other's back.

Quincy was deeply moved by the gesture. He actually felt his knees get weak. When he embraced his son he didn't want to let him go. He hadn't held QJ in his arms since he was a child. If he could have frozen time and basked in the moment for another ten minutes he would have done just that.

Eventually, Quincy was able to pry himself away from QJ. He walked out of the room and followed Lawana into the living room.

"Well, the time has come," said Lawana as she sat on the sofa.

"What's up?"

"I just spoke to Carmen."

"About what?"

"About you."

"What?"

"You heard me. I spoke to her about you. We were talking about QJ returning home, but I used the discussion as an opportunity to bring up your name."

Quincy started shaking his head.

"Don't shake your head," said Lawana. "I wanted to gauge how receptive she would be to talking to you. We would never know if I hadn't asked her some straight forward questions."

"Okay, Sherlock Holmes. What did you discover?"

"I discovered a couple of things. The first thing is that there is still a soft spot for you in her heart. The second thing I discovered is that she is still hurt by the way you left."

"Any suggestions? I don't even know how to approach her. Hell, I don't even know if I should."

"Well, I told her that QJ has been asking about you often. I told her how curious QJ is about getting to know you."

"What did she say?"

"I can tell it had an impact on her. How much of an impact, I don't know."

"Based on the way I left, there is no way she is going to believe I still love QJ, or her."

"Maybe I can help," said QJ, as he stood a few feet away. He'd been eavesdropping on their conversation. "I will talk to her and not get mad. I will let her know that I need you to come around."

"Thanks, son," Quincy replied and smiled. "I'm gonna need all the help I can get."

"As far as moving Terry out of the picture, you're on your own with that one. I will be rooting for you because I can't stand the sight of that fool."

"Trust me, your mother is aware of that," said Lawana. "Since you like to eavesdrop on grown folk conversations, I'm gonna ask you a point blank question."

"I ain't scared," replied QJ.

"Smart ass! How would you feel if your mom and dad got back together after all of these years?"

QJ leaned against the wall. He had a comfort level that suggested he was anticipating that question. The cocky teenager looked at Lawana and then at his father. Like a seasoned actor, he paused for affect although he already had the answer to the question cued up and ready to spew.

"Well?" Lawana asked, eager to hear his answer.

"I think it's a good idea," QJ replied as he stared directly into his father's eyes. "The sooner the better."

CHAPTER 17

JUDGEMENT DAY

Quincy's hands trembled as he stood outside the house he'd purchased for his family twelve years earlier. Carmen had done a pretty good job maintaining the yard, but he noticed that the house could use some touch-up paint in a few places.

To the left of the house, located in the center of the front lawn, was a huge Crape Myrtle. He could remember the day he'd purchased it. Carmen didn't want to plant the tree — she couldn't see Quincy's vision. No matter how much he tried to explain to her that the tree would grow and sprout beautiful bright pink flowers on the branches, she wasn't convinced. Even when he explained to her that the flowers would better accentuate the pink tinted bricks they'd chosen for the front of their house, she ignored him. Eventually he pulled rank, and planted the tree anyway. He was glad to see his vision for the tree became a reality.

Quincy was overcome with a sense of pride, but he knew he'd feel even more proud if he could reclaim his family. He'd been given pep talks by Brotha Nelson, Scoop, Lawana, and even his once rebellious son. Now it was up to him to carry out the mission.

From his peripheral vision, Quincy could see the curtains in an upstairs window shimmy. That was QJ's bedroom. He knew his son was sitting up their silently hoping that things would go as planned.

Quincy saw Terry's SUV parked in the driveway. The car looked expensive. Fancier than any car he'd ever owned. Nevertheless, Quincy knew he'd come too far to turn back now. If Carmen was going to choose to stay with Terry, Quincy was going to put up a good fight.

His steps towards the front door were slow and deliberate. He felt like he was in one of the scenes from a Spike Lee movie when everything around the character is moving, but the character is standing still.

A journey of a thousand miles begins with the first step. Quincy thought to himself. Unfortunately, that journey from the sidewalk to Carmen's front steps seemed a lot longer than a thousand miles.

Rather than focusing on the positives of this monumental decision, Quincy couldn't help but think about all that happened between he and Carmen over the years and the potential negatives that could come from this unannounced visit.

What if Carmen rejects me? I know that I was wrong for leaving her, but I hope she understands that I was sick. Drugs and alcohol were the only things that gave me comfort after she broke my heart. She probably thinks I don't love my son, but that's not true. I do love QJ. And I still love her.

As he walked past the driver side door of Terry's SUV, his negative thoughts increased.

I should probably turn around. Nawh, fuck that! This may be my only shot. Besides, I ain't tryin' to go inside. I just need to convince her to come outside and talk to me for a few minutes. Terry is just gonna have to deal with my presence. If he wants to fight me, I'm ready for that. My family is worth fighting for.

It was clear that Quincy had a lot of catching up to do when it came to income. Still, Terry's car was impressive and expensive.

One things for sure, this ma'fucka must be making good money. I'm wearing borrowed clothing and carrying these flimsy-ass lilies. I'll bet Terry buys her roses every week.

This car looks familiar...and hella expensive.

A million thoughts raced around Quincy's head like race cars at the Daytona 500. His firm chest expanded and collapsed as he took in one last deep breath. His eyes closed slowly as he said a quick silent prayer; hoping to summon the courage needed to ring the doorbell.

What if I've waited too long and Carmen is no longer attracted to me? Father, please, please, please, let this go well for me. I just want an opportunity to say I'm sorry. Father, I want my family back. Please let this be the first step. Amen.

With his last request for God's assistance on its way to the heavens, Quincy extended his finger and pressed the doorbell. His palms were so sweaty that he quickly rubbed them on his pants legs.

Carmen's footsteps could be heard getting closer and closer to the front door. Quincy remembered how much he hated when Carmen slid her feet across the floor when she walked. It sounded like she was walking on sand. Now the sound that once drove him crazy was music to his ears.

Carmen looked through the peep hole, but Quincy intentionally blocked his face with the flowers. She unlocked and opened the door naively thinking that it was a delivery man holding flowers that had been purchased by Terry.

"Oh, how pretty!" she exclaimed as she opened the door—smiling from ear to ear.

Quincy moved the flowers to the side as he displayed an equally large smile. "Hey, Cookie! It's me, Quincy."

Carmen's stomach immediately started churning. The way she frowned, you would have thought she'd been punched in the gut by Mike Tyson. She had an anguished look on her face—like someone who was in desperate need of a toilet after eating collard greens.

"Quincy? Is that you?" she managed to ask.

"Yeah, baby. It's me, Quincy...the love of your life," Quincy replied as he tried to maintain that air of confidence.

Quincy bravely stood at the door and waited for Carmen's response. After a few seconds of awkward silence he finally got a response. But it wasn't the one he expected.

Without forewarning, Carmen punched Quincy so hard it sounded like an adult man clapping his hands. Quincy's knees buckled. He dropped the flowers and immediately placed his hand over his eye. He bent over for a few seconds as he tried to disperse the stars that were now floating around his head.

When Quincy finally looked up his eye was watering and his vision was blurry. He was so delirious that he thought he saw two Carmen's.

Carmen, on the other hand, had a look of pure rage in her eyes. She was preparing to hit him again, but was distracted by Terry's voice.

"Who is that at the door, baby?" Terry asked.

"Uhh, no one," she nervously replied. "Just some man who had the wrong address."

Quincy's eye felt like it was on fire. "Okay," he said finally. "I deserved that."

"You're damn right you deserved it you son of a bitch," said Carmen in a tone filled with anger, but low enough that Terry couldn't hear. "What makes you think you can just come here to my house unannounced after all these years? I don't want to ever see you again you fucking deadbeat."

Carmen's words and tone stung. They stung like the stinger on a pissed off bumble bee. Like salt in an open wound. Like the switch his grandmother used to make him get when she wanted to whip his ass.

What baffled Quincy even more was that Carmen's reaction was a far cry from what Lawana lead him to believe it might be. Lawana never said Carmen would embrace him with open arms, but she didn't say that Carmen would be combative.

"I didn't think you were still this angry. I thought you were open to talking to me."

"You thought I'd be open to talking to you? Where in the hell did you get that idea?" Carmen asked indignantly, peeking over her shoulder every few seconds to make sure Terry wasn't coming.

"Yeah, Lawana told me..."

"Lawana? You've been talking to Lawana? Wait a minute; have you been in contact with my son?"

"Cookie, he's my son too."

"Correction! He stopped being your son ten years ago when you abandoned us. You left your child without a father. You left your wife without a husband. You left us here to struggle."

The pain in Carmen's voice hurt Quincy to the core. The anguish on her face caused tears to formulate in his eye that had been punched. How do you convince someone you abandoned that you love them? How do you make that person believe that you won't do it again?

The easiest thing for Quincy to do at that moment was to turn and walk away. But before he left he needed to say something.

"Cookie, I'm sorry. I understand that I handled things wrong back then, but I've got my act together again. I kicked my drug habit. I've been clean for a while now. I really do..."

"I don't give a damn what you've done!" Carmen retorted. "I want you to..."

Carmen couldn't finish her response to Quincy because her worst fear came to fruition. She'd been standing at that door a tad bit too long.

"Baby, what's going on?" Terry asked.

Before Carmen could make up a lie, Terry was standing behind her and looking over her shoulder. Carmen glanced at Quincy and tried to tell him to leave with her eyes. Quincy wasn't getting the message. She then glanced back at Terry, and tried to close the door quickly.

Terry grabbed the door and opened it up.

"Who are you?"

Quincy stood there silently for a moment.

"Umm, I'm Quincy."

"Quincy?"

"Yeah, Quincy. I'm QJ's father."

Terry was understandably surprised. "Baby, you told me QJ's father was dead," said Terry, gazing into Carmen's eyes with a puzzled look.

"I can explain," said Carmen. "Close the door so that we can talk."

"Excuse me," Quincy interrupted. "Did you just say, *baby*?"

"Yes, I said baby." Terry replied defensively.

"Who are you?" Quincy asked.

"I'm Terry, and this is my woman."

"But," Quincy mumbled.

"But, what?" Terry asked.

"But, but, you're a woman," said Quincy, looking like he'd just been punched in the stomach and needed to take a shit.

"That's right, I'm a woman. And your ex-wife Carmen is now my woman."

"But, I thought you were a dude. QJ told me..."

"QJ told you what?" asked Terry.

Quincy's mind started to replay the events of the past few months. It wasn't long before he realized that it was he who assumed Terry was a man, but not once did QJ actually say that.

The more he thought about it, he realized that neither QJ or Lawana used the words *he* or *him* when describing Terry.

All Lawana kept saying was how opposed she was to Carmen and Terry's relationship, but she never said why.

Quincy's thoughts were racing. *That's why QJ hated Terry so much. Not only was the boy struggling with the circumstances surrounding my ten year absence, QJ has had to deal with the fact that his mother is in a gay relationship.*

"Oh, shit," Quincy finally mumbled.

"*Oh shit* is right," said Terry, wearing a wife beater. "You lost your woman, to a woman."

Quincy's mouth flew open. He was in a daze. So deep of a daze that he didn't bother to swat away the fly that was buzzing around his lips.

"Look Quincy, Lawana never told me she was talking to you. And she definitely didn't tell me you were talking to QJ. If she had told me that I would have told QJ to stay away from you. I don't appreciate you talking to my child without clearing it with me. We have moved on, and I suggest you do the same."

Quincy stood there stunned. Carmen stood there with tears in her eyes. Terry stood there with a smirk on her face.

QJ was at the bottom of the staircase behind Carmen and Terry with an awkward look on his face. The realization that he'd done his father a terrible disservice by not disclosing his mother's sexuality had sunk in.

In many ways, QJ's avoidance of the topic was Carmen's fault. Carmen and QJ never discussed her sexuality. She announced to him she had feelings for Terry, and that the two of them were going to date each other. That lack of communication angered QJ and set off a string of events that ended with his father being humiliated.

The scene ended with Terry slamming the door in Quincy's face. Quincy slowly backed off of the porch. He took steps backwards until he reached his starting point. It seemed longer than his initial walk up to the front porch.

Quincy turned and headed down the street. But he did pause one last time to look back at the house he'd built. The decision to leave his family was a bad one. Thinking he could get his wife back after ten years and coming to her house unannounced was an even worse decision.

Quincy could hear QJ calling his name.

"Daddy wait!"

The fact that this was the first time Quincy had ever heard his son refer to him as *daddy* wasn't enough to make him turn around. He sped up his pace and then started running. He ran for a few blocks. He didn't want to look back again. In fact, the only thing Quincy wanted to do at that moment was get high.

Lawana and QJ sat in the corner of Tiny's Diner. They looked like two spies swapping secrets as they both sat with their elbows on the table while discussing the disaster that took place.

"She did what?"

"She punched him. I saw the whole thing."

"And what did Terry do?"

"Terry was talkin' shit to my dad," QJ blurted out. Lawana was too caught up in the discussion to even pay attention to the boy's obscenities.

"I wish he would have knocked the shit out of her," said Lawana. "I know your mama is pissed."

"Hell yeah, she's mad. She's mad at my daddy. She's mad at me. And she's mad at you."

"She's mad at me?"

"Yep. I heard her tell Terry, 'Lawana set this shit up!' and sayin' how she was gonna ground me for talkin' to him. That's why I told you to meet me here. I knew she would be trippin' if you came to the house."

"I know Terry was eating that shit up. She just killed two birds with one stone. She knows your mama is gonna probably cut me out of her life, and then turn around and punish you. I know Terry loves this."

"You know it."

"Was Terry mad at your mama for lying about your dad's death?"

"If she was mad she didn't act like it."

"That explains why your mama has been blowing up my phone for the last two days. My neighbor told me she was banging on my door last night. I'm glad I wasn't home."

"Yeah, it's probably a good thing. Was my dad home?"

"Baby, I haven't seen your dad since he left my house to go and talk to your mom. That's been nearly 48 hours."

"You think he went back to the park?" asked QJ.

"I don't know. I hope he didn't."

"Can we go to the park to see if he is over there? The sun doesn't set for another hour or so," asked QJ, a look of desperation on his face.

There was a fear in the child's eyes that she'd never seen before. QJ walked around acting like he didn't care about anything or anybody. This was a different kid.

"Yeah, baby. If we hurry we should be able to get over there in time to walk around."

Lawana and QJ were both silent during their car ride to Palmer Park. They acted as if talking about Quincy's whereabouts would ensure that he'd be lost forever. Finally, QJ broke the silence.

"Can I ask you for a favor?" the boy asked timidly.

"Yeah. What do you need?" Lawana felt so bad about everything that had transpired, she would have purchased QJ a car if he'd asked.

"I was wonderin' if we could stop at Walgreen's."

"Yeah. Why?"

"I wanted to run in and get a Chess board."

"A Chess board."

"Yeah. My dad was teachin' me how to play when we were livin' with you. I figured…"

"Say no more, baby," Lawana interrupted. "I understand."

Lawana made a quick pit stop at Walgreen's. She gave QJ a twenty dollar bill, and told him to hurry. While QJ was in the store, Lawana's cell phone started ringing again—it was Carmen.

"I'm sorry, Cee. But I have no intention on talking to you until I speak to Quincy first," she mumbled. "I need to find out exactly what happened."

QJ came running out of the store within minutes. His sprint combined with Lawana burning rubber out of the parking lot made some of the bystanders wonder if they'd just robbed the store.

When she finally arrived at the park, she drove slowly around the perimeter as she looked for any sight of Quincy. Eventually she parked on a side street that was a few feet away from the tree Quincy used to call home.

The spot was empty. No sign of vagrant life form. No sign of Quincy. QJ exited the car and walked a few feet away, and started talking to two homeless men leaning against a huge empty concrete fountain located in the middle of the park.

He returned a few moments later with a dejected look on his face.

"What did they say?"

"They said they haven't seen him."

"Did they know who you were talkin' about?"

"They acted like they did," said QJ and shrugged his shoulders. "Honestly, they were both drunk. We can't trust what they said."

"Well, I know one other place he may be," said Lawana.

"Where?"

"Hopefully, he went back to that Men's group he was meeting with over at Ebenezer Church."

The sun fell from the sky—replaced by a full moon. Lawana and Quincy pulled up to the front of the church, but were disappointed to see all of the lights off. The house where they held their H.A.B.U. meetings was locked up with no sign of life.

"What is this place?"

"This is the place your father came to when he decided he wanted to get clean and sober. I was hoping that he came back here. He told me about a few positive brotha's he met. I hope he reached out to one of them.

"It's late, baby. We won't find him tonight. I'm going to take you home."

"Okay."

Carmen's block was dark and quiet. The only thing that could be seen as Lawana turned onto the street was the gleam from Terry's rims.

"Look, QJ, I need you to focus. That means no arguments with Terry tonight. I want you to go straight inside, be polite to your mama and Terry, and go to your room. I don't want you saying or doing anything that's gonna get you in trouble."

"I feel you," QJ replied. "You should probably let me out right here. I don't wanna risk you being seen. Truth be told, being caught with you right about now could get me punished."

"That's true. Does your mama work this weekend?"

"Yeah. I think they are doing inventory at the store so she will be leaving early Saturday morning."

"Good. I'm coming to get you then. We will go get some breakfast and then ride around to see if when can find your dad."

"Okay," QJ replied and then gave Lawana a fist bump. "He got out of the car and then stuck his head back in before he closed the door. "I know my mama is mad at you, but I wanna say thank you for tryin' to help out my dad."

"No problem, baby. I owed that to him and you," Lawana replied, her emotions obstructing her ability to speak. "Now, go inside. I love you."

"I love you too," QJ replied.

Chapter 18

The sun was booming Saturday morning. It was nine o'clock and Carmen was walking out the front door just as QJ was rolling over.

"QJ, I'm leaving," Carmen shouted. "I want this house cleaned and those clothes in the dryer folded before I get back this evening."

QJ grabbed his pillow and put it over his head. He was attempting to hide his eyes from the sunlight that was bursting through his bedroom window.

"Alright!" he managed to shout.

The next sound QJ heard was the slamming of the front door. He lay in bed for a few minutes until hunger cramps forced him to get up.

After taking a quick detour to the bathroom, QJ made his way downstairs and grabbed his favorite mixing bowl from the cabinet. He then grabbed an unopened box of Frosted Flakes from the pantry, the largest spoon he could find, and the half gallon of milk from the refrigerator.

I know I'm supposed to meet Lawana, but I gotta get something to eat first.

With a mountain of flakes perched on his spoon, QJ's mouth started to water. But his taste buds would have to wait because the door bell rang.

"Damn, man. Lawana is early."

QJ opened the door without looking through the peep hole. A move he would quickly regret. He was greeted by the last person on earth he was expecting to see.

"What up, fool!" Bookie shouted. "What you doing?"

"What you think I'm doing? I just woke up."

"Your mom's at home?"

"Nawh, she just left."

"Good!" Bookie replied, and then barged inside. "What y'all got in this bitch to eat? A nigga hungry."

By the time QJ had closed the door and walked back into the living room, Bookie was already sitting in the living room eating the bowl of cereal he'd prepared.

"Damn, fool!" QJ yelled, and slapped Bookie across the head.

Bookie laughed and ran around the room while he ate QJ's breakfast. "My bad, dog. A nigga hungry."

"So! I'm hungry too," QJ shouted. "You should have got somethin' to eat at your own house."

"Man, we ain't never got food in that house... too many ma'fuckas livin' there," said Bookie. "Besides, a nigga had a hard night."

"Yeah. What did y'all get into?"

Bookie finished eating the bowl of cereal, and then placed the bowl on the coffee table.

"You greedy ma'fucka," QJ said, and then threw the spoon at Bookie.

"Man, chill out!" Bookie shouted, as he grabbed the remote and turned the television station.

"Man, what are you doing? I was about to watch Sports Center."

"Whatever, man. You can watch that shit anytime. I'm tryin' to see somethin'."

Bookie switched from channel to channel until he found what he was looking for.

"What's up?" QJ asked.

"Shhhh..."

The reporter appeared standing in front of a news van with a brooding look on her face.

We are here in Palmer Park where Crime Scene Investigators are combing the site for clues to another homicide in the city.

"Yeah, this is it. Oh shit, this is it!" Bookie shouted.

"What's up?" QJ asked.

"Man you missed it last night."

"Missed what?"

"I finally caught up with that fool."

"Who?"

"That homeless fool I had the fight with a few months ago. You remember the dude under the bridge.

"Me and Tweety saw him walking down Carrollton Avenue yesterday while we were on the bus. We got off the bus and followed him to the spot where he had his little card board house set up.

"As soon as we saw where he was staying we got on the bus and went to the crib. You know I had to grab my shank. I told you I was gonna get that ma'fucka."

QJ sat there silently. He felt like a live toad was crawling inside of his throat. The reporter was talking, but QJ didn't hear a word the woman said. He was staring at the television, but listening to Bookie.

"What happened?" he finally asked.

"Nigga, what do you think happened? I shanked that fool up last night!" Bookie replied, laughing and beating his chest. "I caught that ma'fucka sittin' on a bench loaded and drunk. He didn't know what hit him.

"I told you I was gonna get that fool back. You know a nigga don't forget shit. He may have thought that shit was over, but it ain't never over until I get my revenge."

QJ continued to sit there quietly. He couldn't speak. He just stared at the television and tried to visualize his father's last moments.

He walked over to the window that faced the front yard. Still no words were uttered. Bookie was still talking —

bragging about the murder. QJ refused to look at his friend. The guilt he felt was too heavy.

"Why didn't you leave that shit alone, Bookie? Now the police are gonna be lookin' for you."

"Man, I ain't worried about the police. You know as well as I do they ain't gonna waste time investigating a murder involving an old bum. Hell, it ain't like somebody is gonna miss him. His family probably doesn't know where he is. I'd be surprised if he even has a family."

QJ didn't reply. He wanted to cry. He wanted to fight. QJ wanted to kill the boy who'd just killed his dad.

Bookie was a budding sociopath. He had no remorse for his actions. All he wanted to do was eat, joke, and brag about his murder.

"Say, dog. Can I go in your room and play your video game?" asked Bookie.

"Yeah," QJ managed to reply. "Go head and get started. I'll be up there in a minute."

QJ walked into the downstairs bathroom located beneath the staircase. He turned on the faucet and then splashed water on his face. His tears were now disguised, but his heart was aching. For years he believed his father was dead only to discover that it was a lie. Now, the lie had become the truth.

QJ exited the bathroom and walked back into the living room area.

"Say dog, I see you got one of those combination Checker and Chess boards up here. Come on up here so I can beat that ass in a game of checkers real quick before I start playing this Play Station!" Bookie shouted.

"I'm coming," QJ replied, as he looked at a steak knife sitting on the kitchen counter.

QJ found himself in the same state of mind he was in the night he beat Terry with the baseball bat. He wanted to inflict pain — the same type of pain that had been inflicted on him. His mind told him to take a deep breath and think, but the pain and guilt inside of him were lobbying for revenge.

QJ walked over to the counter and grabbed the steak knife. While he stared at the knife, his father's voice entered into his mind, *Checkers is reactive, chess requires strategy.*

He could hear his father's voice so clearly that he turned and looked around the house to make sure Quincy wasn't standing there with him. His father's words were echoing repeatedly in his head. So much so, that QJ clutched his forehead.

"Well, hurry up, fool!" Bookie shouted again.

"Wait a second," QJ replied, and then placed the knife back on the counter.

With the weight of his father's death tearing at him, QJ walked over to the corner of the counter and grabbed the cordless phone.

"911. What's your emergency?"

QJ looked out of the kitchen and saw Lawana pull up. "Uh yeah, my name is Quincy Washington Jr. I am the son of the homeless man that was found murdered in Palmer Park last night. His name is Quincy Washington Sr. I called to say that I know who murdered my dad."

"You know the person who murdered your father?"

"Yes. His name is Dexter Howard—we call him Bookie, and he's here in my house right now."

"He's there right now?"

"Yes. He's upstairs in my bedroom waiting for me to come up and play checkers."

"Where are you? Are you safe?"

"Yes. I'm downstairs in the kitchen...playin' chess."

About the Author

Originally from New Orleans, Louisiana, Brian W. Smith is the author of several controversial best-selling novels, including *BEATER*, *Nina's Got a Secret*, and *Mama's Lies – Daddy's Pain*.

Brian is also the owner of Hollygrove Publishing. Visit the company's website at www.hollygrovepublishing.com

To email Brian directly: bsmith@hollygrovepublishing.com or http://www.facebook.com/HollygrovePublishing

Book Club Discussion Questions

This story deals with multiple issues: the break up of a marriage; abandonment; homelessness; parenting, and forgiveness—just to name a few. These questions are designed to tackle several of these issues:

1. Quincy left Carmen after she cheated on him, gave him Chlamydia, and then refused to apologize. Quincy admitted that he made a mistake when he walked away from his son's life. Was he justified in leaving Carmen?

2. If you answered yes to the first question, then this second question is for you. Carmen told QJ when he was very young that his father died. Considering her role in the break-up, and the obvious emotional toll it took on Quincy, was Carmen right or wrong for telling QJ that his father died?

3. Quincy felt compelled to tell "his side" of the story. Do you think he was right or wrong for telling QJ that he left Carmen because she gave him a venereal disease—knowing that it could taint the boy's impression of his mother?

4. While hanging out with his girlfriend, QJ saw Quincy and pretended he didn't know him. If you were driving in a car with your co-workers and saw a homeless relative standing on the side of the road, would you drive past that relative and pretend you don't know him/her or would you stop your car and assist that relative? Be honest—this is a "real" question, designed to elicit "real" comments.

5. Lawana thought she was doing the right thing by telling Carmen she saw Terry in the club with another woman. Should she have made that phone call or remained quiet about what she saw?

6. Quincy got into an argument at his first H.A.B.U. meeting when another attendee called him a *deadbeat*. Do you feel that a man who commits a crime and is subsequently incarcerated is just as much a *deadbeat* as a person who isn't in jail, but blatantly ignores his parental responsibilities?

7. When QJ and Terry had the fight, Carmen sided with Terry—although Terry instigated the fight by grabbing QJ's book bag. How would you have handled that situation?

8. Quincy felt that the circumstances dictated that he sit quietly and accept some of QJ's disrespectful outbursts and reactions. Do you feel he should have been more assertive with the out of control teenager sooner?

9. Do you feel that Lawana set Quincy up for failure or did she do the right thing by trying to help him reclaim his family?

10. If a man abandons his family—regardless if its one month or one year—should the wife allow him to come back and be a part of their life?

Author Comments

As with all of my novels, I tried to take a common everyday occurrence, and create a storyline that would facilitate discussion.

As a proud father of two little boys, I do all I can to be a positive force in their lives. In my opinion, being called a *deadbeat* is the ultimate insult anyone can throw at a man. And although I believe there are many people that deserve the title, I know that life isn't always black and white — there are always gray areas. I wanted to see if I can exploit some of the gray areas inherent in the topic of *deadbeat* dads.

I'm also intrigued by life's day-to-day occurrences. Homelessness is a topic that has always intrigued me. As young impressionable kids, we all grow up with visions of careers we'd like to pursue and lifestyles we'd like to have. But I don't know anyone who dreams of one day being homeless. Writing this book enabled me to fuse my thoughts about both topics: deadbeat and homelessness.

I hope you enjoyed *DEADBEAT* as much as I enjoyed writing the book. If your book club chooses *DEADBEAT* as your Book-of-the-Month, shoot me an email. If I'm in your neck of the woods, I'd love to come to the meeting and hang out with you and your members so that we can discuss the book. If I can't physically be there, maybe we can do a phone conference. Reach out to me. My email address: bsmith@hollygrovepublishing.com.

Thanks again for your support.

Brian W. Smith

Other novels by best selling author, Brian W. Smith

- **The S.W.A.P. Game**
- **Mama's Lies – Daddy's Pain**
- **Donna's Dilemma**
- **Final Fling**
- **Nina's Got a Secret**
- **Donna's Comeback**
- **My Husband's Love Child**
- **Beater**

www.hollygrovepublishing.com